WOMEN OF THE YEAR

A Collection of Short Stories

KAREN RICHARD

GusGus Press • Bedazzled Ink Publishing
Fairfield, California

© 2016 Karen Richard

All rights reserved. No part of this publication may be reproduced or transmitted in any means, electronic or mechanical, without permission in writing from the publisher.

978-1-943837-34-2 paperback
978-1-943837-35-9 ebook

Cover Design
by
DESIGNS

GusGus Press
a division of
Bedazzled Ink Publishing Company
Fairfield, California
http://www.bedazzledink.com

WOMEN OF THE YEAR

To my wife Pam,
who believes in me more than anyone else.

Acknowledgments

A book is the product of more than just the author, even though there is only one name on the front. This book is no exception. I had the pleasure of being a part of a writing group on Facebook that brought in published authors to critique our work. Some of those stories are a part of this book so I would like to thank the authors who generously contributed their time, Isabella, Linda Kay Silva, Karelia Stetz-Waters, Melissa Braydon, Lacey Gardner, Saxon Bennett, and especially Sandra Moran. The online members of that group gave me support and encouragement when I needed it, especially Kim Johnson, Gena Ratcliff, and Dani Dixon Bradshaw. Love you guys. The GCLS Writers Academy taught me so much and I appreciate everyone associated with it. A more wonderful group of writers would be hard to imagine. My beta reader, cheerleader, and all around buddy from across the pond, Jody Klaire was invaluable in getting these stories perfected. She makes me a better writer. A big thank you to Bedazzled Ink for making me a part of the Bink family. So many fantastic writers have come through your pages and I could not be prouder to be a part of the newest imprint, GusGus Press. And finally, thanks to my wife Pam who puts up with time away from her devoted to author stuff. Marrying you was the best thing I ever did.

Contents

January · 11
42 Years

February · 23
Mitchell's

March · 37
Pie's Puppy

April · 49
What a Way to Spend My Birthday

May · 57
CUL8R

June · 63
June 26, 2013

July · 71
Girlfriend Glasses Versus Wife Eyes

August · 83
Kelly

September · 105
DBAP

October · 113
Companion

November · 127
I See You

December · 149
Honor Flight

January

42 Years
January 22, 2015

I GLANCED AT the digital clock on the nightstand. It was almost time to leave. I stuffed a nondescript grey hoodie and large dark glasses into the cheap duffle bag and paused to gently untangle the wires before loading the most important item. I zipped the bag closed, stood slowly, grabbed my cane, and limped out of the house. I had everything I needed for today's mission.

I drove to the parking lot near the clinic. Today was the 42nd anniversary of the Roe v. Wade decision, so I knew there would be plenty of people around. It didn't matter which party put a president in the big white house, we were a people deeply divided on the issue of abortion. Our new Congress had started off the session by introducing a bill seeking to ban abortions after twenty weeks in the House of Representatives. The newly Republican Senate promised to introduce a companion bill as well.

I was here today to make my position known, to draw my line in the sand. I was not the only one with that idea. There was a huge crowd of pro-life people standing outside the clinic holding lurid signs with pictures of bloody babies. Young children, too young to know why they were there, holding signs saying, "I'm glad my mommy didn't abort me." There was another group that were getting as close as possible to the people entering the clinic, shouting questions like, "Are you going to kill your baby today?" Opposing them was another cadre of earnest-looking people whose sole purpose was to keep the protesters at the legally mandated minimum distance from the front doors of the business. They had repainted the lines on the sidewalk yesterday to make sure they were bright and noticeable. And there was one cop, leaning up against his car, sipping on his Starbucks cup. He seemed above the drama playing out in front of him.

I saw a young lady chugging along in a beat-up old Chevy Cavalier with flaking grey paint. The car spluttered a few times before the engine shut off. I cautiously approached her as she eyed the crowd of people in front of the clinic.

"Are you going to the clinic?" I tried to keep my voice low, calm and shield her from viewing the crowd.

Her eyes flicked over my face, worry filling them before she nodded as if in defeat. "Yes."

I unzipped the bag, reached in, and pushed a button.

Suddenly sound exploded from the ear buds, the appropriate-to-the-day lyrics of Green Day's "American Idiot" exhorting us not to be controlled by the media.

"Hey," I said softly, "if you don't like Green Day I have other stuff on the iPod. It just needs to be loud enough to drown out the yelling. There is nothing people across the street have to say that you need to hear."

She wouldn't meet my eyes. "No, Green Day is fine."

I gave her the grey hoodie and dark glasses to put on.

"Don't look anywhere but at your feet and don't turn off the music until we get inside the building and the doors are closed. They are not allowed to touch you." I looked at the crowd, which seemed to have grown since I arrived. They were definitely louder or maybe they just felt more aggressive since I knew we were going to be the object of their vitriol in a few short minutes.

"The buffer zones around the clinic used to be much larger." As I thought about buffer zones I got mad all over again. It seemed like for every step forward in preserving a woman's right to choose, like safe zones, a step or two backward seemed to occur, like the forced pre-abortion ultrasound laws. "Anyway, thanks to last year's Supreme Court decision on Massachusetts's law, a thirty-five foot buffer zone was declared unconstitutional." I smacked my cane against the asphalt.

The girl jumped back in alarm.

I softened my voice and tried to explain. "It makes me so mad that a lot of municipalities are not enforcing the buffer zones that are on the books. The lines mark the fifteen feet." I glared at the one cop leaning against his squad car looking like he would rather be anywhere else.

"I'm Kelsey by the way. What's your name?"

"I'm Brittney just like fifteen other girls I went to school with. The only special thing about me is that I managed to get pregnant the first time I had sex."

After that brief flash of personality, Brittney hunched her shoulders and lowered her eyes but not before I caught the shimmer of a tear just swimming in the corner of her eye. She started to reach for the handle of her car as if she was changing her mind about being here. "I'm scared."

"Are you scared to go in the clinic or are you scared about what happens after that?" I asked.

She seemed to almost shrink in on herself. "A little of both."

"Well, let's take care of one thing at a time. First we'll get in the building then we can talk, okay?" I have never been a touchy-feely kind of person. My modus operandi was action, not feeling, but I reached one arm out to Brittney and gave her an awkward one-armed hug to try and reassure her.

She fell into my arms and the tears that had threatened before flowed in earnest. I stroked her back and made reassuring noises like I would to a scared animal. I don't know how long we stood there but she seemed to draw strength from my embrace.

"Sorry about breaking down. I haven't really had a minute to feel anything since I found out I was," she gulped and her voice dropped, "pregnant." She straightened her shoulders and visibly gathered herself almost as if saying the word pregnant brought her focus back. "I guess we should get going. Won't you be able to hear them yelling?" she asked as she took the iPod.

"Don't worry about me. I'm used to people yelling at me." Before I retired I had negotiated labor contracts. My entire job was having people yell at me.

She put on the headphones, adjusted the volume so that I could feel the bass throbbing in the center of my chest, pulled the hood up over her head, and hooked her arm through mine. We walked across the street my right arm linked with her left arm. I held my cane in my left hand. If there was any trouble I could use the cane for more than support in walking.

An older man in the crowd noticed us. I could tell the minute he identified us as potential patrons of the clinic as his eyes glittered with a religious fervor of a preacher who found a nonbeliever to hear his proselytizing. As the members of the horde surrounding him caught his excitement, they turned their focus to us. They flapped signs, images of dead babies flashed at us. A young girl ran at Brittney, fingers spread to grasp for her. I stuck my cane in front of the child to stop her progress.

I turned to her mother. "Keep your child back or we will sue you and her for assault, assault and battery in civil court at least."

The mother rolled her eyes and mumbled half under her breath, "What else could I expect from a baby killer?"

"Back away right now or I will have McGruff the Crime Dog over there," I pointed to the uninterested police officer, "arrest you on criminal charges."

The mother grabbed her child and pulled her back. We didn't stop. Didn't look up. Brittney didn't flinch. The loudspeaker boomed with some idiot's hellfire and damnation speech.

One elderly lady approached Brittney. "Can I speak to you before you kill your baby?"

I was glad that the music was loud enough to drown that out. Ten short steps away were the stairs to the clinic entrance. We traversed those steps and grabbed the door handles as the shouts of the individual mob members became more and more strident.

Finally we made it inside. The cacophony of voices was drowned out by the heavy doors that shuttered the clinic. As we walked toward the reception desk Brittney asked if we could chat a minute after we checked in.

We moved to a little alcove that provided a modicum of privacy. Brittney perched on the edge of the chair and hesitantly asked me if she was doing the right thing.

"There is no way I can answer that for you."

I stared into the distance. I remembered forty-five years ago when I'd sat on a folding chair in someone's kitchen. He'd performed a "procedure" on my little sister who had gone to him seeking to terminate her pregnancy. I had taken her to that back alley butcher which resulted in her death. I was too young and naïve then to save her or really do anything other than mourn. Now I was willing put myself on the line to make sure women continued to be able to exercise their right to choose.

"You have to make that choice on your own."

"Well, my mom wanted to drive me here today to make sure I did it." She looked down, again failing to meet my eyes. "I'm only sixteen and she doesn't want to raise her grandbaby or have me ruin my chances of going to college or even finishing high school. I had to skip school to make my appointment today." She appeared fascinated by the poster hanging on the wall of the alcove detailing a woman's reproductive system.

"Well, it's hard to raise a child and go to school but there have been plenty of people that do it. It requires a great deal of maturity and commitment though." I glanced around the clinic. They sure didn't spend money on interior decoration. The cinder block walls were painted in a sickly industrial green and the cheap brown commercial carpeting was frayed and showing its age.

"Jason, the father, he wants me to have an abortion because he doesn't want to pay child support." Brittney finally turned to look at me. "He had the nerve to ask me if I was sure the baby was even his." Her jaw was clenched as she spat out the words. Her voice cracked with this admission of his betrayal. "His mother wants a grandchild so bad she doesn't care what it takes. But she won't be the one taking care of the baby." Her face reflected the indecision in her voice. "She was on the phone with me last night begging me to keep the baby." She chewed on a fingernail. "And my dad . . . well . . . my dad just told me that he didn't want any bastards running around his house and if I kept the baby I better look for a new place to live."

My heart broke in half at that gut punch from her father. My dad had thrown me out at seventeen, although for very different reasons. "Sounds like you have a lot of people telling you what they think you should do and no one asking you what you want. What do you want, Brittney?"

"I am too young to raise a child, so for me it's either an abortion or adoption. I just know I can't keep the baby myself." She looked me in the eyes. "What would you do? I mean if you were me?"

"To tell the truth, I'm a lesbian so unplanned pregnancies are not really an issue." No matter how often I came out to someone, and I had done it hundreds of times over the course of my life, I always expected a negative reaction. Maybe not as negative as my father disowning me but I never expected something good.

Brittney smiled at my admission. "I figured that out by looking at you. Uh, I didn't mean that in a bad way. I have gay friends. Oh crap, I'm making it worse. I couldn't care less about someone's sexuality. I'm just glad you are here for me."

She was so stinking cute tripping over her words while trying not to offend. This was by far the best reaction I had ever had to coming out. Maybe I needed to start spending more time with people her age because Brittney was awfully open and accepting. It kind of renewed my faith in her generation.

"Pregnancies take a lot of planning. I believe that every woman has the right to consider all the options and make the decision that is best for her, not best for the father or his wallet, her mother or anyone else." I shifted in my seat. This damn chair was hard on my old bones. But really even sitting for a few minutes caused my leg to stiffen up. "It is really a question of allowing a woman to make an informed choice. So I can't tell you what I would do." I leaned forward in my chair. "I can say this, I really wish there was no need for abortions."

I wished that people had to work as hard as lesbians and gay men to get pregnant so that every child was wanted. I wished there was a foolproof method of birth control and that anyone who wasn't ready to have a kid used it to protect themselves from pregnancy and disease. "Until that day comes I just want to make sure women are not deprived of the ability to choose or scared away from clinics."

"Well, thanks for being the first person to ask me what I wanted instead of telling me what to do." Brittney chewed on another fingernail and shifted in her seat. Her nails were all bitten down to the quick. "If I just ask the staff for more information today will you escort me in if I decide to come back?"

"Of course I will. Just call the hotline and tell them you want me to be your escort."

Brittney sighed and relaxed her shoulders. "Okay, thanks. I haven't decided yet."

A door opened and Brittney jumped a little as the sound echoed through the waiting area.

"Brittney Foster?" a woman in scrubs called out.

She turned and gave me a hug. "Thank you . . ." Tears welled up in her eyes again as she turned to leave.

"Anytime."

She headed for the door to the examining rooms.

"Hey, let me give you my number in case you want to talk some more." I put my name and number into her phone and hoped she would call if she needed me.

I watched her walk through the door and I sent up a plea to the universe. It would almost be a prayer if I only believed in God. A plea that whatever decision Brittney made that she would be at peace with herself and her choices. And, that women everywhere continued to be able to choose, so no one ever lost her little sister because of a botched abortion.

February

Mitchell's

I HEARD A herd of elephants trampling down the hall of the rehab facility where I was staying while recovering from my knee surgery. Oh, wait, it was just my granddaughter, Heather, running down the hall to visit me. She burst into the room and flung herself into my arms to give me a huge hug. She was a blond-haired blue-eyed thirteen-year-old whirlwind. She had not yet hit the terrible teens and visiting her grandmother in the rehab facility was still enjoyable, unlike the last time her sister had visited. Not that Brittney minded visiting me, but to a sixteen year old, sitting in a small room while her mother criticized her hair, clothes, and friends was a teenage version of hell.

"Hey, Heathen, where's Brittney?"

"Gaga, quit calling me heathen, my name is Heather. And Britt is in trouble for something. No one will tell me what it is but she's been grounded for a couple of weeks already."

She jumped up and collapsed in the chair next to me, appearing to have no bones as she flung one leg over the arm of the chair. The facility was set up to look as little like a hospital as possible, so the chairs were overstuffed and seemed to encourage family and friends to stay and visit for a while. The room was homier but still resembled a high-end hotel room more than my house. I missed having my stuff around me, the memories of my life at my fingertips.

"Gaga, tell me about your first kiss." Heather sat up straight and leaned in toward me with a serious look on her face. "How did you know that she wanted to kiss you? Or did you kiss her?" Her leg bounced up and down as she waited for my answer.

"Why would you want to hear about that ancient history?" I shifted a pillow under my knee and raised the footrest in my chair a little higher as I thought about how to answer her.

Heather's leg started bouncing even faster as her cheeks turned red and she looked away. "Well, Gaga, there is someone I met that I think I want to kiss and . . ."

She was off and running about her latest crush as only a young teenage girl could do and my mind wound back to Baltimore in 1979.

I STOOD NEXT to my best friend, Nancy, on the corner of Pratt and Exeter in the pale light of the lone street lamp. Halfway down the street was a dark, unlit door. We were teammates on the swim team, volleyball team, and softball team at our high school. You would think that at a small high school the odds of finding another lesbian would be slim, but we met in the locker room our freshman year and had been best friends ever since.

Unfortunately, and contrary to what most of our other teammates believed, we were just friends. There was no spark between us romantically. Nancy was always sighing after the hippie girls in their wrap-around skirts and earth shoes and I was more into the butch ones. I had never met a butch girl in real life but this weekend, tonight I hoped, that was going to change. I knew I wanted a female version of the bad boy, with a fast car or better yet a motorcycle.

I slowed my steps as we looked down the street. "Are you sure we're in the right place? And I'm not sure about how I am dressed." I looked down at my Levi's and Converse tennis shoes. "What if they are all wearing disco outfits from *Saturday Night Fever*?"

"You look great. Yes, I'm sure this is the right place. Quit trying to get out of this. We've been planning this since Christmas break and we aren't leaving without going in." Nancy was great at talking me into doing stuff and keeping me on the path.

I was a little on the shy side and Nancy pushed me out of my comfort zone. Of course, I talked her out of her crazier schemes so we balanced each other out. That balance was why we were standing near a gay bar in Baltimore instead of on a train to New York City to hang out in the Village. Nancy only came up to my shoulder but she was a tough-looking girl. She wore a beat-up pair of black motorcycle boots and some well-worn jeans and a flannel shirt. Her Dorothy Hamill haircut was at odds with her clothing but it worked for her.

"Are you sure the car is going to be safe parked there? I would hate to have to try and explain to my dad why we were in this part of town when he thinks we are at the Valentine's Day dance."

I turned as if to head back to the car and Nancy grabbed the flipped-up collar of my rugby shirt to stop me.

"Nope, you are not chickening out. Look, I have heard it's not a big deal, we just go up to the door and they buzz us in."

Sure, not a big deal, just a lesbian bar. Why should I be nervous? My parents had no idea I liked girls much less that I was twenty-five miles away from our small town, in the city, in a scary part of the city. I started to hyperventilate a little bit. Nancy smacked me on the arm.

"Relax, they don't check id's so we just have walk up like we belong there. C'mon, we can do this."

A cute little butch walked past us. In painted-on Levi's and a leather motorcycle jacket, she was obviously headed to Mitchell's. My eyes followed her confident, sexy stride. Nancy turned me and gave me a little push toward the bar. We walked up to a nondescript black door. The bass from the dance music pounded and rattled my sternum. I heard the harsh sound of the buzzer and pulled the door open.

The large woman just inside the door glared at us and held out her hand. She looked like every stereotype for a lesbian I had ever read about. Her arms were tattooed and a lit cigarette hung from the corner of her mouth. Her hair was short and slicked back like the Fonz from Happy Days. I must have looked confused or maybe scared because she sneered and pointed at the hand written sign saying two dollar cover Saturday and Sunday. Nancy handed over a crumpled five dollar bill and told me I could buy her a drink inside.

As I walked in, my heart pounded like it was trying to escape my chest. To the left was a bar and to the right a postage stamp sized dance floor. The size didn't deter this crowd though as they were crammed together, hands in the air, grooving to the beat. I caught sight of two women grinding against each other. I stopped dead in my tracks to watch. Nancy grabbed my arm and pulled me to a small table.

"Quit staring like it's the first time you ever saw lesbians," she hissed. "You don't want to look like it's your first time in a gay bar."

"But it is my first time, and yours too, unless you have been holding out on me." I almost tripped as I was too busy looking at all the women to watch my step. I had never been in one place with so many women and not a guy to be seen. I didn't know where to look or not look. I wanted to take it all in but didn't want to look uncool. I settled for stuffing my hands in my pockets to hide the shaking.

"You know I've never been here but this girl I was talking to at work told me about this place." She glanced around the small bar. "I was hoping she would be here tonight because she was really cute."

"You're such a slut."

"You're just jealous."

We settled in the uncomfortable chairs and I turned my attention back to the dance floor. The two women I had spotted when we walked in were no longer pretending to dance. One woman was backed into a corner and the other woman appeared to be examining her throat, using her tongue. I couldn't look away and a flurry of butterflies started floating through my midsection. I had only imagined two women kissing and here were two, right in front of me doing more than kissing.

I kept watching as the woman on the outside reached between the two of them. I am not sure what she did but the woman on the inside seemed to like it as she reached around, grabbed the other woman's ass and pulled her closer.

As soon as we sat down a cute girl in a too-short-for-the-cold-weather skirt approached our table. Nancy pulled out of her habitual slouch and looked her up and down. Trying to be cool, she ordered a scotch on the rocks. When the waitress asked what kind I waited for Nancy to falter and be shown up as a fraud. She calmly asked for whatever the rail was. I was impressed. It seemed almost as if she had been here before or at least in a bar. I asked for a draft beer. I tried to catch Nancy's attention as the waitress walked away but Nancy could only focus on the waitress, well, on the sway of her hips and the smooth firm muscles in her legs. Okay, I was looking too. I couldn't believe that a couple of sixteen year olds were able to get away with coming to a bar and ordering drinks but that was Club Mitchell's. If you had the money they would serve you.

I asked Nancy if she had been here before but she pretended she couldn't hear me. I punched her in the shoulder. Hey, she deserved it for obviously going to a gay bar without me. She was way too comfortable for it to be her first time. As we waited for our drinks I couldn't help but glance at the dance floor.

I sat facing the dance floor, trying to remember every detail of my first ever exposure to seeing women together. It was thrilling and a little scary. I was no longer flirting with the possibility of kissing a girl, I was sitting in a place with a lot of girls that I could potentially kiss. The fluttering in my stomach that started when I had walked in got even stronger. The longer I stared at the couples on the dance floor the stronger it got. I couldn't keep staring but I couldn't look away.

Just then the DJ started playing "YMCA" by the Village People. Nancy and I jumped up to dance. That was one thing I was comfortable with. I practiced enough at home in front of the mirror, at least until my dad yelled at me to turn that, "crap you called music," down. We pushed our way on to the dance floor, singing along to the music and forming the letters with our arms.

I felt hands on my hips and someone behind me pulled me back into her. I didn't know who it was. The only person I knew in the bar, in fact the only gay person I knew at all, was Nancy.

This was definitely not her, two soft breasts pushed into my back as the mystery person grinded herself against my ass. I was slowly being moved off the dance floor and into a dark corner. The owner of the soft breasts turned me around and backed me into a wall. It's a good thing the wall was there because I could hardly hold myself up. The butterflies were nothing compared to the flock of birds taking wing inside me when she inserted her denim clad thigh between my legs.

She pushed against me. All the blood in my body headed south. My mouth was too dry. I couldn't speak. She bent down and brushed her lips against my ear. In a husky voice she said, "You're new here, aren't you?"

I just nodded. The ability to speak seemed to have deserted me. She chuckled low and deep and I could feel the vibration of her laugh everywhere she touched me.

"Good, I like fresh meat."

Before I could even process what she meant or what she was saying, her lips captured mine. Her tongue demanded, no commanded, my mouth. I had never been kissed before, not a real kiss, not like this. Even in my wildest dreams. I never imagined that I would turn into liquid. It was a good thing she pinned me to the wall because my legs were incapable of holding me up. She swept her tongue through my mouth. I vaguely felt her hands running up my sides. I had no awareness of my surroundings and didn't care that we were in public. As her hands moved to my breasts I could feel my nipples getting harder. I grew wetter. I was physically incapable of stopping, swept away in a rush of hormones, cigarette smoke, and alcohol.

She moved away. Left me barely standing against the wall. I forced my eyes open. Another woman pushed her away. I couldn't hear what they were saying over the music, the blood rushing to my head and my own heartbeat. The interloper leaned in toward me, took my elbow, and pulled me away from the wall and toward the door.

As we stepped outside in the cold February air, my sanity returned and my cheeks grew hot. I contemplated what I had been doing, or about to do, in front of all those people.

I turned toward my rescuer, who stood about four or five inches taller than my five-foot-six. She had short hair and jeans that hugged her muscular legs. Her t-shirt was stretched, tight, across her chest. The sleeves were rolled up to show off her well-defined biceps. She clapped her hand on my shoulder. "Relax, kid, I'm doing you a favor. Sandy is kind of a vulture."

I was still kind of in a daze as I glanced up at my rescuer, a butch in shiny leather. I looked back at the ground, embarrassed by my behavior. I took in at her highly polished boots and the muscular legs encased in tight denim.

"She swoops in on the new kids and takes advantage." She put her hand under my chin so I would look her in the eye. "Let me give you some advice, don't come alone, if you set your drink down get a new one and remember . . . you are in a public place."

My face grew hot again and I looked back at the ground, hoping for a hole to open up and swallow me. "Thanks for stepping in. I kind of lost my head for a minute. I guess I owe you one." I thrust out my hand and noticed it was shaking. "I'm Shawn by the way."

"Pleased to meet you, Shawn, I'm Kelsey." She took my hand and smoothly shook it and shot me a grin that took my breath away.

Nancy came running out the door of Mitchell's and stepped between Kelsey and me. She pushed me back behind so she could stand between us. She sneered at Kelsey and stood up tall, trying to appear bigger than she was. I could see Kelsey trying not to smile at Nancy but there was no way that Kelsey was intimidated since she was six inches taller and a good bit bulkier than Nancy.

I loved Nancy for her fierce defense of me. That's why she was my best friend, bar none.

Kelsey held her hands up in a placating manner and backed away from Nancy. "Easy there. I was just offering your friend here some words of wisdom."

"Like don't leave the bar with someone you don't know?" she retorted as she thrust her chin out and put her hands on her hips.

"It's okay, Nance, she was actually helping. C'mon. Let's go back in." I put my arm around her and gently pulled her back toward the door. "This time don't close your eyes on the dance floor okay?" I winked at her as we moved back in to Mitchell's.

Nancy was still glaring at Kelsey. "Are you sure you're okay? I looked around and saw this one," she jerked her chin at Kelsey, "dragging you outside."

"I am fine. C'mon, let's go back in." I tried to distract Nancy as we moved away. "Did your cute girl show up?"

I turned back to Kelsey and thanked her again for saving me from being *that* girl, the one who would be forever remembered for an indiscretion on the dance floor.

"No big deal, kid. But let me tell you, I know kissing a girl is awesome." She smiled and winked at me. "And it's really freeing to be some place where that is okay." She frowned a bit. "But don't lose your head to your hormones. As electrifying and sexy as that kiss was, a kiss is even better when you care for the person you're kissing."

MY RECOLLECTION WAS interrupted as my daughter Dana, Heather's mom, walked into the room. She glared at me for all she was worth. "Heather, go get something to drink from the vending machine."

She handed Heather a few dollars. "Nothing with sugar or caffeine for your grandmother."

Heather thundered down the hall in the direction of the Coke machine with all the subtlety of a marauding rhinoceros.

"Were you seriously just telling my thirteen-year-old daughter the story of your first kiss, the one where you swiped the car, went into the city, and lied to your parents . . . *and* almost had sex in public?" She said it as though she were chastising one of the kids in her elementary classroom.

"Slow your roll there, Dana. I didn't give her all the details just the important stuff like how getting to know the person first is better."

Heather poked her head in the room. "And that even lesbians have to kiss a few frogs to meet their Princess Charming!"

March

Pie's Puppy

MY NAME IS Pie, well, my nickname anyway. It is totally dorky but my dad is a mathematician and it was his idea of a joke because I was born on March 14th, you know 3.14, mathematical pi. I cannot begin to tell you the ways I have suffered due to my name. Believe me I have heard every version of, "can I get a piece of your pie," and more variations of, "are you cherry?" than any one person should have to hear. Fortunately, my mom convinced him that listing 3.1415 on my birth certificate would be a mistake. She was always the more practical of the two of them.

He was a math professor at the University of Wisconsin in Madison. His head was always in the clouds or formulas or theoretical numbers, or something so boring, I quit listening. My mom was an English teacher. She taught British Romanticism with an emphasis in Scottish literature at the same university. So she convinced him to name me Bridie. Bridie is a small savory Scottish pie that no one has ever heard of so most people don't make the connection. It could have been worse I suppose, they could have named me Cherry or Peaches.

I went by Pie. It was easier to let people think it was just a random nickname that stuck instead of a carefully thought out combination of the passions of my parents. I guess I was kind of that too but I really don't want to think about that aspect of my parent's life.

You would think with college professors for parents that I would be some kind of intellectual but that seems to have skipped this generation. I was an only child and only too aware of how I had disappointed them. One great thing about living in Madison, aside from the four seasons of weather and the four lakes surrounding the town, was that it was a paragon of liberal thought in the otherwise conservative state of Wisconsin. I think that was due to the influx of college students every year that increased the population of the city by almost twenty percent each August. Whatever the reason, the city was liberal, open, and accepting. Those qualities are why coming out as a lesbian in Madison was about as easy as it gets in the Midwest. So, while my lack of intellectual curiosity and pursuit of higher education disappointed my parents, the fact that I was a lesbian was no big deal.

Since I wasn't the scholar my parents wished me to be, I had to find a career that didn't require a college degree. Fresh out of high school, I took the exam to work for the Post Office and was hired as a letter carrier rather than working inside sorting the mail. I enjoyed being outside for most of the work day even though the Madison winters could be brutal. I started out as a part-timer, as everyone did, but I got to substitute for all the carriers in the so-called "Lavender Ghetto" on the east side of Madison. It was where it seemed like most of the lesbians in Madison lived, probably because of the proximity to the Willy Street Coop. (That's the cooperative grocery store on Williamson Street.) I liked to go there for lunch when I was working a route in the area. They had really great sandwiches and salads and all the women that worked the deli counter were cute and flirtatious.

It was one of those rare but perfect days in March where it was sunny and warm and summer was promising to appear soon. Siren that she was, summer didn't sing of the humidity or the mosquitoes when she enticed you with her melodies of long sunny days and hot steamy nights. But this was March and the first brave flowers were poking through the still brown lawns as I walked down Jenifer Street delivering the mail. It was too chilly for shorts but I had left my jacket in the mail truck and was enjoying my time in the sun. If I timed it right, I would be near the Coop at lunch time. I was lost in thought as I wondered who would be the lucky recipient of my always awkward but hopefully amusing lunch time flirtations.

I had just made my delivery to Marquette Elementary School and was delivering to the houses on Jenifer Street across from the school playground, when ahead of me I spotted a flash of light brown, low to the ground. It was an animal of some kind but I didn't get a very good look as the owner of the fur ran between two houses. I strolled up the driveway to see what it was and heard a small whimpering noise coming from behind a shed. I knew that mailmen and dogs were supposed to be mortal enemies but I always carried treats in my mailbag to offer as a bribe in case I ran into one who was less than friendly.

As I carefully rounded the corner, I saw a small ball of blonde fur cowering against the side of the shed, shaking like me before I handed my parents my report card. I knelt down so I wouldn't seem so big and scary and spoke soft and low, extending my hand. The tiny pup lifted her head up and cautiously sniffed my hand. I inched closer but she backed away, trying to crawl under the shed. I put the mail bag down and sat on the ground. I broke off a small piece of a dog treat and tossed it on the ground, halfway between us. I couldn't see if she was a girl, we weren't that close yet. Since some of my favorite blondes were women, I was going to think of her that way until I could prove otherwise.

Oh, she wanted that treat but clearly her short life had given her plenty of reason to mistrust people and few, if any, reasons to trust us. Her tiny nose was sniffing as hard as she could and she did a puppy shuffle to get closer to the treat. (The kind where the dog doesn't seem to move at all but suddenly she is on the carpet or the couch or the bed). That move inched her closer and closer to the treat until she could extend her tongue just far enough to wrap it around the treat and haul it back into her mouth. She crunched on it quickly, almost swallowing it whole and then looked up at me hopefully. I put another piece of a treat on the ground closer to me. She shuffled a bit closer. Before too long she was next to me happily crunching as I petted her. I spent most of my lunch break getting to know her, and yes, confirming she was a she. Her light brown fur was short except around her ears which was matted and tangled. She was very small, no more than ten pounds and skinny, too skinny. Her ribs stuck out and it was clear that she had not been eating regularly. When I scratched one floppy ear, her back foot started thumping against the ground. When I paused in my petting, she stuck her nose under my hand as if to encourage me to continue. As I sat there on the cold ground talking to her, she crawled up on my lap, and licked my nose. Her stubby little tail was only an inch long and when she wagged it back and forth her whole back end moved.

She didn't have a collar and was clearly a stray. We bonded in the sunshine by the shed for a few more minutes then I carefully carried her toward my mail truck. I didn't really have a plan for what to do with her while I finished working but I didn't want to take the chance on her running away and not being able to find her once I finished. I walked by Mrs. Smith, who was sitting in her yard enjoying the sun.

"What in the world do you have there?"

"Oh, I found this puppy when I was delivering the mail. I'm trying to figure out what to do with her while I finish up work."

Mrs. Smith was a fixture in the neighborhood. She considered it her duty to keep an eye on everything and everyone that came and went. When the snow kept her inside the house she sat by the window peering through the curtains. When I delivered the mail I would see the curtain twitch as she watched me walking by. During the heat wave last summer she met me at her mailbox with an ice-cold glass of water. This winter it was hot chocolate with marshmallows. Every letter carrier dreams of a customer like Mrs. Smith. Like a lot of the older people in the neighborhood the arrival of the mail was an important part of the day so I always made sure to deliver her mail before I took my morning break.

Mrs. Smith had obviously been clearing out her flowerbeds as there was a pile of leaves and trash that the winter winds had blown in beside her bench. Her hands were gnarled and bent with arthritis but she still did her own yard work. When she fell behind I would stop by after work to help her. In addition to the upkeep on her house, she provided after school care for her two grandchildren, Brittney and Heather, who had recently moved back to Madison with their mom, Dana. I got all the gossip over hot chocolate and water. I opened the gate to her fenced-in yard and plopped down next to her on the bench, still holding on to my newly acquired fur ball.

"Well, she sure is a scrawny mess, isn't she?"

I looked down into the brown trusting eyes of my pup, saw past her matted fur, the too prominent ribs and backbone that marked her short life to date. "She may not be much to look at but I bet she cleans up real nice. Can I leave her in your yard until after work? I promise I'll be back no later than five. I need to finish the route and get some supplies then I'll come get her."

Mrs. Smith held her hand out to allow the pup to get a sniff. "That'll be okay but if you don't come get her I'll call the pound. Brittney and

Heather will be here after school and they can play with her and keep her out of trouble. Now set her down and let her explore the yard a bit. She'll be fine."

"I better get moving then." I looked my new puppy in the eyes and promised her I would be back. I set her down and she immediately started whining but I quickly shut the gate and turned away. I really didn't want to leave her but I knew the sooner I finished my route, the sooner I could get back.

I really hustled that day, skipping lunch at the Coop in my eagerness to pick up my puppy. I had other priorities now. She needed a name, I couldn't keep thinking of her as the puppy. Since the schoolyard was like a park, I was going to see how she felt about the name Parker.

I headed back to the post office to punch out and ran by the Coop to get some dog food, flea shampoo, and other supplies before heading back to Mrs. Smith's house. As I pulled up to the house, I didn't see my new girl in the yard.

My heart sank. What if she had misbehaved and Mrs. Smith decided to call the pound anyway? I dashed up to the front door with my heart in my throat. I rang the bell and heard the loud stomping of two kids running around inside like a herd of elephants. Mrs. Smith opened the door.

"Hello, dearie, come on in. I had to bring your dog in the house because she kept escaping under the fence, trying to follow you. I put her in a cat carrier until the grandkids got home from school." Mrs. Smith motioned me inside. "They've been playing with her all afternoon and I think she is completely done in." She walked into the living room and took her customary seat by the window. "You can borrow the carrier if you need it to get her home."

"Oh, Mrs. Smith, thanks so much for watching her. Sorry if she put you out at all. I will return the carrier tomorrow," I said as I picked it up and headed for the door.

I was anxious to get Parker home and see how she did in my apartment. I looked inside the crate to see Parker curled up in a ball snoring softly. She must have been tired, she didn't even move when I shut the car door.

Because Parker had been living in the elements I decided a bath was in order so when we got home I plopped her in the tub. She seemed really unsure about the whole water thing but she definitely liked the part where I rubbed her all over even if it did make her smell funny.

Once I got her cleaned up and fed, she was even cuter than I thought at first. Her fur was a light blonde, almost white. She had ears that seemed too big for her face and her fur was still that soft puppy fuzz. She had a little stub of a tail that seemed to move a hundred miles an hour when she was excited. And she was clearly not potty trained. Fortunately, my apartment was the first floor of a house and had a fenced-in yard right outside the back door. I let her outside while I set about cleaning up the puppy piddle. Good thing the floors were all hardwood. I heard little yips and the sound of tiny puppy claws scratching at the back door.

"Hold your horses, Parker. I have to clean

up this mess before I let you in to make another one," I called out to her (as if she could hear, and understand me).

The yips and scratches stopped. *Wow,* I thought. *She is super smart.*

I heard renewed scratches, this time at the front door, the door that wasn't inside the fenced-in yard. Parker had escaped from the back yard and thoughtfully came around to the front door so I could let her in there. I was rethinking her name. Maybe I should call her Parker-dini since she was clearly an escape artist to rival Harry Houdini.

I opened the front door and she bounced in with a proud look on her pint-sized puppy face. I knew from this point on it was going to be Pie and Parker. I looked at her and made her a promise, although I had no control over what happened before I came into her life, I was going to do everything in my power to make sure the rest of her life was everything a dog could want.

And, it was.

April

What a Way to Spend my Birthday

MY NAME IS Devyn Donavon but everyone called me DD. You would've thought that my nickname was based on my initials or perhaps the size of my chest but you would be wrong. Way wrong, as in could not be further from the truth. I wasn't dubbed DD until I was thirty, prior to that I was called Dona Juan as a play on my last name and the number of girls I'd dated. The real reason had a lot to do with my birthday and what a way to spend my birthday it had been. I was trudging home after another ten-hour work day, a short day for me, since I had started my new business, Two Dykes and A Truck.

I would have rather spent it raising a glass with friends, but no, I'd decided to start this business to secure the future for my family. My live-in girlfriend, Brandi, and I wanted to have kids one day but not until we were a bit more financially secure. We had been together for four years. I had finally settled down and could not be happier. This relationship was different from all the ones I had in the past. Maybe because we actually dated before we moved in together.

My business model was based on lesbians that followed the more familiar path of bringing a U-Haul to their second date and, so far, was pretty successful. Since most businesses failed in the first year I was working a lot of hours, putting the time in to make this venture succeed.

Brandi had probably planned a surprise party for me since she thought turning thirty was a big deal. I really hoped not because I was not a surprise kind of girl. Predictable was my middle name and I had been called boring by more than one of my exes. I was a Prius in a world of Maserati's, dependable, solid and unexciting.

The houses in my neighborhood were large single-family houses that had been built in the early 1900s. Many of them had been converted into apartments but our small two-story rental wasn't large enough to break into more than one unit. Our house looked like an afterthought in the neighborhood and was more utilitarian than decorative. Most of the nearby houses had Victorian flourishes like bay or stained glass decorative windows. Our house was functional rather than beautiful. It did the job without a lot of panache. The other houses had lovely landscaping, trellises with climbing roses that looked as though the blooms were color coordinated to the trim of the house. Our house had a few evergreen shrubs along the front but neither Brandi nor I had a green thumb so the shrubs were the antithesis of the highly regimented ones that lined the property of our neighbors. It was mid-April so spring was finally coming to our Midwestern town. Well, as much spring as we ever had, it was really usually tulips then summer. But I did enjoy the spring flowers that added a pop of color to the neighborhood. Our house had a few volunteer blooms that seemed to have migrated from the neighbor's yard and I had managed not to kill with my anti-plant magic. But other than that our house stood out for its ordinariness.

As I walked up my street, I noticed that the first-floor lights were all off but there was a dim glow from the upstairs bedroom that seemed to be flickering. It was way too early for Brandi to be in bed since she kept late hours so I suspected when I opened the front door a bunch of people would jump out and yell Happy Birthday.

I hiked from the bus stop, practicing making a "oh my gosh, I am so stunned that you threw a party for me" face. I'm not a good actress so I wasn't sure I would be able to pull it off but if Brandi went to the trouble to gather people in honor of my birthday, I was going to express my appreciation.

I climbed the stairs and crossed the porch as I listened for small sounds that would give away the surprise. I inserted my key and flung the door open with the look I perfected firmly affixed to my face. I was greeted by dead silence. Hmm, seemed as though I was all wrong, there was no party, but why was Brandi upstairs already?

"Brandi, where are you?"

Silence. I glanced up the stairs. The bedroom door was cracked just enough that I could see the candlelight flickering. My heart was racing. She's waiting up there for me, ready to give me my birthday present. God, it had been so long since we'd been intimate that I could feel myself start to get excited. The light from the front porch shone through the window and onto the stairs.

I looked at the stairs. I spied something small and silver sitting on the riser. It was a Hershey kiss, right in the center of the stairs. Three steps up was another one . . . Brandi had left a trail for me to follow, the little vixen.

As I climbed the stairs, I decided to dial up a surprise of my own. I made a slight detour to the hall closet where we had stashed the toy box the last time her mother came to visit and we were "straightening" up the house. It was a time in history where lesbians were just starting to live openly but Brandi was still not ready to be out to her parents. So, when her mom came to town we moved all my stuff out of our room into the other bedroom, hid the naked lady wall art, boxed up the lesbian books, and moved the toy box to the linen closet under the flannel sheets.

I grabbed a few things from the closet and slipped into the bathroom. If Brandi was going to give me a birthday present I was going to give as good as I got, in my birthday suit. I stripped off my work clothes and put on my leather harness and her favorite neon purple dildo. I took a quick look at myself in the mirror. I wasn't sure what Brandi saw in me, I was an ordinary run-of-the-mill butch with short spiky hair and she was a striking willowy blonde who could have had her choice of women. But she chose me and I was bound and determined to keep her happy in every way.

I snuck out of the bathroom and flung open the bedroom door wearing nothing but a strap on and a smile. Suddenly the lights came on and all my friends jumped out and yelled, "Surprise!"

Suffice it to say that I didn't have to use the look I practiced on the way home as the terror and surprise on my face was genuine. I discovered that you don't die from embarrassment, even when you are literally bare-assed. Henceforth my birthday, at least among our crowd, was forever known as Dildo Day and my new nickname was DD.

May

CUL8R

I EASED ONE foot out from under the covers and carefully placed it on the floor. The breathing from the opposite side of the bed remained steady as I slipped out and grabbed my clothes from the floor where I apparently flung them with abandon the previous night. Where the hell was my underwear? Oh shit, they had ended up on a chair across the room. I had a vague memory of my companion from the previous night pulling them off and flinging them over her head. I fled to the bathroom. I have got to stop doing this. Every time I go home with someone from the bar I end up staring at myself in some stranger's mirror wondering how my life turned into such a hot mess. I grabbed my phone to see if I was somewhat close to my apartment or if I was going to have to Uber home.

"Oh shit," I muttered.

Someone had appropriated my phone while I was on the dance floor and had taken pictures of me trying to twerk. My ass really didn't move that way but after a few shots of Jaeger I sure thought it did. I slipped into last night's club outfit and tiptoed through the studio apartment, not taking a full breath until I was outside the door. Another walk of shame for me. Fortunately for me my club attire was not obviously something that was evening wear only. Since it was May in the city, I usually wore jeans and a tank top.

It got hot working it on the dance floor, in more ways than one. Plus, I worked hard to develop my upper body and the tank showed that off. It had the added advantage of showing off the tattoo on my right shoulder of a pinup girl. It was done in a real 40s style but back then she would have been riding a missile and on the arm of someone in the service. She would also have had clothes on. My version had a big busted naked girl riding a vibrator. Hey, when my friends and I went out dancing it had the added advantage of keeping the boys away and drawing the more adventurous girls closer.

I hit the street and looked around, not immediately recognizing any landmarks. I pulled up the Uber app and sat on the front steps of the brownstone to wait. I decided to check Facebook while I waited and noticed that I had been tagged in a bunch of photos taken at the club. I was so engrossed in the pictures that I didn't notice when the Uber driver pulled up until she honked at me.

As I got in I recognized a face in the background of one of the club pics. It was the evil ex who had photobombed me. I was surprised that her face could actually be photographed since she was such a soul-sucking vampire. Wasn't the legend that they couldn't be seen in mirrors or pictures? I was glad that I hadn't seen her, or at least that I didn't remember seeing her last night. There probably would have been a scene with her trying to get me to pay attention to her and me ignoring her or going off on her.

I guess I wasn't cut out for relationships.

Women of the Year

They always seemed to want more from me than I could give. Even though the whole one night stand thing was getting old it was still better than being trapped in a relationship with someone who was not what she pretended to be when we met. I may not be the sharpest tool in the shed but if you take my money for my share of the rent and bills and the power gets turned off and an eviction notice gets posted on the door of our apartment, I think I get the message that I am being used.

Just then my phone buzzed with an incoming text from Stacey. Who the hell was Stacey? *Hey U sexy thing, where u run off 2 so early. I want 2 start the day the way we end the night.*

Oh great, my one night stand had my number and the belief that this was going to be more than a one night stand. I had to shut that down fast. As I looked through the text history I realized we had been sexting while we were in the club last night so the old wrong number dodge wouldn't work. My phone buzzed again.

Cmon back.your cute.

I texted back. *My cute what?*

Huh?

I am sorry I can't spend time with someone who cannot text in complete words with capital letters and the proper use of the word you're. It's not you, it's me.

And with that I blocked her number. I may be a bit of a slut but I had my standards when it came to the English language.

June

June 26, 2013

I SLAPPED MY hand down on the highly polished boardroom table and shouted, "What the hell just happened?"

All the young sycophants jumped slightly at the sound. They were not used to any display of emotion from me at all. I had been heading up this Republican think tank for the past twenty years. Of course, it didn't hurt that my father had wanted me to have a behind the scenes role in the political arena since he knew I would never pass even the most surface background check much less the sort of scrutiny that political candidates underwent these days. It didn't really matter to me, I preferred the role of puppet master anyway, and this role did not require that I hide the sexual activities that most of my clients would consider deviant . . . those that weren't titillated that is. I did like the ladies.

As I stared down the table, I spoke in a much more measured tone. "We need to find a new way to attack this liberal takeover of the traditional role of marriage. I want ideas at a mandatory staff meeting scheduled for eight a.m. tomorrow." As I gathered my briefcase and headed for my office I pointed at my administrative assistant. "My office, ten minutes." I knew he was planning to leave after this meeting but I needed him for my next set of meetings. It wasn't all sunshine and roses working for me, but all my former aides, at least the ones who hadn't been fired for gross incompetence, had gone on to be very successful in state or national politics, so they were all willing to put up with the long hours. Ten minutes gave him just enough time to grab a stale sandwich from the vending machine and order some fresh coffee for me.

As I entered my office I instructed my secretary Betty to get Dick on the phone. And yes, she was a secretary, she typed and answered the phone, none of this administrative assistant bullshit for me. A few minutes later the phone buzzed and it was Betty telling me she had Dick on the phone. I hit the speaker button. "Dick, you son of a bitch, I blame you for this. That speech in 2009 at the National Press Club where you told everyone that people ought to be free to enter into any kind of union they wish, any kind of arrangement they wish. That the way marriage has been regulated is at a state level. It's always been a state issue, and you said that's the way it ought to be handled today."

I ran my fingers through my hair and continued my tirade. "That opened the doors for the state of California to do exactly that, only look where it all ended up today. Then last year you were encouraging Maryland state legislators to vote to legalize same-sex marriage." I tapped the Bluetooth in my ear to switch to the hands-free. I needed to walk while I was thinking. "Look, just because your daughter is a fucking queer doesn't mean you need to support it. What happened to the old fashioned way of dealing with homos in prominent political families? You disowned them or sent them into the priesthood or found another way to keep it hidden." I snickered to myself when I said that because my father had done that exact thing, relegating me to a single-issue think tank that had become a major player in conservative politics. "When you speak the way you have since you left office, there is a direct line to the decision that damned liberal court made today. You have to start laying low on the social issues."

I paced up and down in my spacious corner office, running my hands through my hair. "And what is this Senate rumor with your other daughter, the normal one? I've been hearing she was feeling out the incumbent, to get him to step down so she can run. I see problems. I don't think Mike is ready to step down yet so you better get her under control."

"You don't have any daughters do you?" Dick asked.

"Nope, no kids, but if I did they wouldn't be running the show the way yours appear to. But back to the point, what the hell happened today?"

"Look," he replied, "California is not my fault. That, that god-damned German governor wouldn't defend the law."

"I think he's Austrian but all the foreigners sound the same don't they? And anyway, I took care of him, didn't I?" Once he and his attorney general declined to defend the Prop 8, I sent out some private eyes to get the goods on him. It took me almost nine months but the story of his peccadillos with the housekeeper eventually broke in the *LA Times* five weeks ago. That was going to end his marriage and his political career. Why he wanted to be married to someone from such a prominent family of Democrats is beyond me.

"Yes, well, is there something you want from me?" Dick asked.

"Yes, I want to know what the hell you are going to do about this wrong-headed decision."

"I don't know if I agree that it is wrong."

"Look, I really don't care who marries who but as long as the liberals are fighting for gay marriage it keeps their focus off the real issue, the fact that our party keeps screwing the little guy to line the pockets of the rich." I paused as the office door opened and my assistant entered bringing in my coffee.

I motioned to the conference table in the corner and he set the mug down there. I pointed to a chair by my desk and he sat down waiting for me to finish my conversation.

"As long as the liberals have another target to focus on we can keep protecting the so-called one percent. I need you to start thinking about another issue to get the liberals fired up about. If we don't take over the message and point them the way we want who knows what those fools will grab next to fire up their idiots but it will probably involve raising taxes on the rich."

"What about some more war on women stuff? Maybe I can get another one of these Tea Party assholes to make an anti-abortion comment."

"I'm not sure that will work this time. It needs to be something bigger than a race in congress that won't even shift the balance of power. We need something that will have a long-term impact."

"Can't those fancy interns in your think tank come up with something?" Dick asked.

"I can't let them know the real goal. They have to stay focused on the purported mission of my group, we are a right-to-life think tank so most of them are single minded in their approach to politics, abortion bad, babies good. Well, let me know if you come up with anything. It has to be big. I still can't believe that we lost the challenge to a law signed by that horny hypocritical Bubba. I thought we had enough bi-partisan credibility to make sure that at least the DOMA claim would fail."

"I gotta go. I'll do some thinking about a distraction issue and call you tomorrow."

All I heard was the dial tone as Dick hung up. I guess that was some kind of one-upsmanship in hanging up first but I didn't care. All I wanted was an issue to displace further economic scrutiny. Suddenly it came to me and I strode to the office door and yelled to my secretary, "Hey, Betty, get the president of Hobby Lobby on the phone."

July

Girlfriend Glasses Versus Wife Eyes

STANDING IN THE hallway, I watched her smack the hospital bed in frustration. I paused for just a moment to get my face in order. It hurt me to see my wife in pain and it was even worse when the pain was more than physical. Oh, the physical was bad enough. Actually it was horrible, life-altering injuries caused by an IED at a time when all the troops were supposed to have been out of Iraq. The politicals and press had made such a big deal out of the end of the war in Iraq in December of 2011. All the troops were out by then but my wife Brenda was sent back in June of 2014 to defend against ISIL or ISIS or whatever they were called. She was not back there even two weeks when it happened.

An IED exploded under her truck, well the truck she was driving anyway. She flew from the vehicle and suffered a concussion and lost her left leg. Huh, lost her leg makes it sound so benign, like misplaced keys or sunglasses. Her leg was shattered and had to be amputated above the knee. So, here we were at an Army hospital. She was working on her recovery and I was working on keeping a positive attitude. We had been in the service for years. Well, technically she was the only one in the service and I was a military spouse but we also serve who sit at home.

When Brenda first joined the service, well before I met her, the infamous Don't Ask, Don't

Tell program was in place. Although it was better than the previous policy of rooting out and dishonorably discharging the evil and scary homosexuals from the service it was far from what gay and lesbian advocates had hoped for from President Clinton. I first met Brenda at a gay bar in DC in 2003.

I SAW HER through the clouds of smoke that tended to permeate every gay bar I had ever been in. I noticed her from the time she had first entered, marching in like she owned the place. I knew she was military or maybe ex-military based on the way she stood. Of course there were a lot of people in the bar that were affiliated with the military since this was the closest gay bar to the Pentagon. Equally obviously none of them were in uniform since showing up here dressed that way would presumably violate the "tell" part of don't ask, don't tell. It would be flaunting sexuality in a way that the armed service wouldn't accept. I always played a little game with myself when new people walked in, military or civilian and if Army or Marine, their rank and Military Occupational Specialty or MOS. The government floated on a sea of acronyms and paperwork after all.

In any event when I saw Brenda across the bar I really didn't care about any of that. She stood tall and strong, not quite at attention but not exactly at ease either. It seemed as though she was drawing on what she knew to feel comfortable in this environment. She had entered with a group of people but she stood by herself. I was intrigued by her looks and bearing but there was no way I was going to get involved with someone in the military. But that didn't stop me from walking over to her.

"Hey there. Army right?"

She looked at me suspiciously, like I was an undercover operative out to get the gays out of the military. "Hello."

"Relax," I replied. "I don't work for the Army. In fact, I am a journalist. My name is Amy."

Instead of putting her at ease, she moved from parade rest to full on attention, everything but the salute. I could almost feel the tension radiating from her.

"Ma'am, I don't know what you are trying to do here but I really don't want to talk to anybody from the press. Nothing personal, Ma'am."

"Clearly I am not from any branch of the service since I don't have that whole stick up the ass way of standing. Nor do I punctuate every sentence with an excessive use of the word sir or ma'am." I moved a little closer to her and half rested on the nearby barstool. I waved my hand at the bartender and asked for another beer. "Can I buy you one?"

"Ma'am, I can get . . ."

"You can get over calling me ma'am and tell me what you are drinking." I reached for the beer in her hand and turned the label so I could see it. I pointed to the bottle and asked the bartender for one of those as well. "Relax for just a minute, okay? I am not on duty tonight, not looking for a story, not looking for a girlfriend, just looking for a drink and someone to drink with. So, what's your name, and before you give me a fake name, let me just say that I really am just looking for a friend, not a source."

"Okay, I guess." She moved to the bar stool next to mine and sat down. "I'm Brenda."

AND THAT BEGAN a friendship that would last for the next five years. It lasted through her serial military girlfriends. They all seemed fine but I never thought any of them were good enough for her. The relationships all ended when one or the other got deployed or moved or even when Brenda or the girlfriend of the moment underwent a background check and feared the relationship would become a matter of record. Our friendship lasted through my four-year relationship with Taylor. When Taylor broke up with me, it was Brenda who comforted me. And a year after that it was Brenda, sitting on my couch, catching me up on her latest deployment and the trials and tribulations of combat communications, who suddenly stopped, leaned over, and delivered a toe curling kiss.

Our relationship was different from any one I had been in before. Maybe because we were friends first, maybe because we spent a significant period of time apart when she was overseas or maybe because it's always different when you find the one who was made for you. In any event, in September 2011, when the DADT policy was officially overturned Brenda got down on one knee and asked me to marry her. It was incredibly romantic. She was on temporary duty to the Pentagon and I was still living in the DC area. Since she was off duty she was able to wear civilian clothes as we strolled around the monuments in DC. At the steps in front of the Lincoln Memorial with the reflecting pool shimmering from the light of the almost full moon she dropped to one knee and took my hand.

"Amy, since I met you I have become better. A better friend, a better girlfriend, and a better person. You make me want to be the best version of myself. Your unwavering belief in me makes me believe I can do anything. More than anything else I want to go through the rest of my life with you by my side. Would you do me the honor of becoming my wife?"

I was floored. I had thought that perhaps we might end up there someday but those thoughts were fleeting (and to be honest mostly after we had mind-blowing sex). But I never suspected, never expected to see my love on one knee. I was rendered mute, the love welling up in me and spilling out. I don't know how long I stood there, silent, staring at the ring in her hand but it must have been an interminable length of time for her.

She shifted uncomfortably on her knee. "Amy?"

"Yes, yes, a thousand times yes!"

"Whew, you were so quiet you had me worried that this was not where you saw us going."

"I do, I mean yes but this was completely unexpected. When do you want to do it?"

She raised an eyebrow at me. "I always want to do it with you but if you mean get married, I am on TDY in DC for the next month so we can go down and get the license anytime. Unless you want a big ceremony we can apply for a civil ceremony at the same time and do the deed before I finish up this assignment in DC."

We headed back to my apartment, discussing our future plans and trying to remember all the details of joining our lives together. Three weeks later we had a simple ceremony in front of the court clerk although we each wrote vows to the other.

I started crying when we got the paperwork and sobbed through the entire ceremony. I just never pictured myself getting married. I know a lot of girls and women who dream about this day but that was never me. I knew from a young age that I was a lesbian. Marriage was not something that was on my radar.

Now that I was actually getting married and to the woman of my dreams I was overwhelmed with all the feelings. But we got through it. And we were looking forward to being together as the troop withdrawal from Iraq was scheduled to be completed in a couple of months. Brenda was thinking about her career plans after the Army but she wanted to put in a few more years first. If only we had known . . .

YEP, IT'S ALWAYS that last one, you know when you have one drink too many, you go from just fine to over the top? It was the same with Brenda's last deployment. We had been married for almost three years and had managed to spend most of that time in the same place but then she was deployed back to Iraq in June of 2014. And that is where she was when the IED went off and blew off her leg and how we ended up in this place. I fixed my face and went into her room.

"Get out, please. I don't want you to see me like this," she said.

"See you like what?" I moved over to her left side and took her hand. "Alive? Bren, when I got that call I was so scared. All they told me was you had been hurt."

She wouldn't look at me and stared down at where her left leg had been. "Look, I can't do this. I don't want to see you. I don't want you around me, or what's left of me. I contacted a lawyer to draw up the paperwork. I want a divorce."

The force of her words were like knives to my chest. I couldn't understand what she was asking for. I loved her. Her injury didn't change that. I tried to tell her that but when she said the word divorce I pulled away. She took that as agreement with her ridiculous request.

"It's better this way. You don't want to be saddled with a cripple. We wouldn't be able to do all the things we used to do before. I won't be that active woman you fell in love with and I won't ask you to settle for what's left of me."

I grabbed her hand again and put my fingers under her chin to make her look at me. "Bren, you have been wrong about things in the past but you have never been so wrong. I married you, the person you are on the inside, my loving, beautiful, funny, irreverent, sarcastic wife. None of the things I fell in love with were located in your leg. Everything I love about you is still here." I moved my hand to her chest. "In your heart."

"Ames, I know you think that now but putting

up with a cripple is not something I would ask my girlfriend to do."

"And maybe a girlfriend wouldn't do it. But I am your wife and I see you, as the person who makes my life better by being in it. Maybe other people who have come and gone in your life have only seen you through girlfriend goggles and that was fine for them. But I see you with a wife's eyes and nothing is ever going to change that."

That was five years ago and it was hard at times and easier at times but we found our path together.

August

Kelly

I WIPED HER brow to maintain some kind of contact. No reaction, no change in the quiet yet intrusive beep of the heart monitor. No sharp intake of breath, just the steady whisper of the machine keeping the other half of my heart tethered to this earth.

It had only been a few weeks and the doctors remained positive, but I struggled to do the same. The shell occupying room 352 bed 2 at Memorial Hospital was not my wife, Kelly. It looked like her but with her eyes closed I couldn't see the intelligence and humor that made her green eyes sparkle. I fooled myself at first, imagining she was only asleep. But now I grasped at straws, praying to a god I never believed in. Situational faith is not faith at all. Wishing on a star, stepping over all the cracks in the sidewalk—they all yielded the same result . . . the steady beep of the heart monitor, the gentle whoosh of the breathing machine.

Why? Why had she stopped there for her morning coffee? There's a fucking 7-11 on every corner between our house and her work. But she was fearless and reckless and bold and I knew it had been going on longer than she had admitted.

"It's no big deal, I'm not afraid of some bullies who get their jollies by calling me names. They are just jerks who aren't worth my time."

Kelly picked her keys up off the counter and jangled them back and forth. I could tell by the set of her jaw, the way she clenched and unclenched her teeth, that something was upsetting her. Usually she was reserved in the morning and pretty low-key before she stopped for her morning coffee on the way to work. But this morning, this particular morning she could not be still. Even when she stood facing me, her leg bounced with nervous energy. Her body seemed coiled with a reserved power usually seen in a caged animal as they paced back and forth. She was dressed for work in her business casual attire, khakis and a long-sleeved blouse. Her short hair was gelled and spiked to sharp points and the short cut emphasized her angular jaw and pronounced cheek bones. Androgynous, strong, sexy, and confident. I unconsciously licked my lips as I contemplated how good she looked.

"Well, what did they call you?"

I stepped into her space and put my arms loosely around her waist. She twisted away as though being confined by my arms was too much to bear. She turned away from me and strode across the small kitchen and into the dining room.

"That's not important. The important thing is that I will not be intimidated into changing my behavior. I am going back to the store to get my coffee every morning and if those two guys are there and want to start something I will stand up for myself."

I followed her toward the bedroom. It seemed like she and I were talking about two different things and I was scrambling to keep up my end of the conversation. We started off with me asking her what her work schedule looked like as I came home from my mandatory night shift. I hated when I had to rotate to working nights because I always felt out of step with the rest of the world. This seemed different though. It wasn't just my over-caffeinated up-all-night-but-it's-time-to-sleep brain. There was something else going on and I needed to figure this out before she left for work.

"What do you mean stand up for yourself? I don't like the way this conversation is going. I want you to be safe and not go looking for a fight."

I walked up to her and gently cupped her cheek with my hand. Her cheeks were flushed and her eyes flashed with anger. While I was glad her anger was not directed at me, not this time, I was still confused. She leaned into my hand as if to draw strength from the contact.

"Please, baby, just get your coffee somewhere else."

She whirled around and resumed her pacing from room to room in our small house. I trailed behind her, still feeling both emotionally and physically out of step. I was not sure where her anger was coming from. But she was angry, she raised her voice, turned to face me, and emphatically stated, "I am not going to let a couple of men push me around. If I avoid getting my coffee there then they win." She turned again and headed back toward the bedroom.

"Wait a minute, back up. All I got from that was that there were two guys making rude comments when you stopped for coffee yesterday

morning... what did they say?" I turned to follow her again, feeling like a baby duckling trailing behind its mom. I grabbed at her belt loop so she wouldn't feel trapped but needing to feel a connection. I really needed to wrap my arms around her, tame her angry mood, and get her to slow down and tell me what was going on. Kelly was a doer not a talker. She didn't process and endlessly discuss her feelings. I knew she loved me, I felt it way deep in my soul. I told her often that I loved her, never casually or thoughtlessly. But Kelly preferred to show me in little ways, taking me to my favorite pizza place, even though I knew she preferred another place, or picking up some flowers for me for no special reason. *"I think this is more than you are telling me."*

"Well, for the past two weeks . . ."

"Two weeks, this has been going on for two weeks and you are just now telling me? What the fuck baby?" Now I turned my back to Kelly and paced back and forth. I wrapped my arms around myself.

"Don't yell at me, I was going to tell you, I am telling you now. I knew you would overreact." The tables had turned and now Kelly was trying to calm me down. I was not a yeller, I rarely raised my voice so the fact that I was yelling now put Kelly on notice that she had done something wrong.

"But, honey, this has been going on for two weeks, whatever this is." I took a deep breath and stopped pacing, trying to calm down. I again cupped her cheek. I pulled her close and wrapped my arms around her. She leaned in, drawing

strength or calmness from me, centering herself. "Can you begin at the beginning please . . . two weeks ago you stopped to get coffee. You parked in the parking lot and then what happened?"

"I went in and got my coffee and on the way back to the car this guy in a black pickup truck started calling me a carpet-munching dyke." She pulled out of my hug, her temporary calm vanished. Off and pacing again toward the kitchen, she suddenly turned, her feet shoulder-width apart, her arms crossed and a fierce look on her face, as though she were facing down an enemy. *"And I am going to go back and get my coffee there or they win."*

"What do they win? What do they win if you patronize another coffee spot and don't go looking for a fight with them?" I heaved a deep sigh and crossed my arms, feeling defensive and protective and confused all at once.

"They win the feeling that it is okay to yell at people and get them to change their behavior because they don't like the way someone looks." She picked up her keys from the side table. Her keys were on a keychain with a rainbow heart that I had given her so she would always know she had my heart with her. *" . . . or the clothes they wear, or the color of their skin, or the fact that they wear a head covering or attend the synagogue."* She pulled on her shoes. She ran her hand through her hair to push it out of her green eyes as she glared up at me. *"They win that their behavior is acceptable in this society and it is not."* She turned and put her hands on her hips like I was the one attacking her. *"I will not be bullied. I will*

not be pushed around." She scowled and ripped her leather motorcycle jacket off the hook. *"I am going to stand up for myself and for all the other people that these man have intimidated, yelled at, or even looked at funny."* She yanked open the door, then stopped. She turned and fixed me with her hardest stare. *"And I am not looking for a fight. I am just going to tell him that if carpet muncher is the best he can come up with then his prejudice is far outweighed by his ignorance."*

Thinking back on it I am sure that her response was not that temperate. In fact witnesses later confirmed that she had actually been called no-good lousy dyke and her response was something along the lines of, "Bravo Captain Obvious, got it partially right, I am a lesbian but what's it to you? Did your last girlfriend leave you for another woman causing your man-sized ego to shrivel up to the size of your dick?" But that was not what she said then, she claimed her response would be measured, that she would not go looking for a fight . . .

"I wish you wouldn't. I wish you would just go to another store." My voice dropped. I was no longer yelling or upset but really scared. I wanted to demand that she not confront these jackasses but telling Kelly she couldn't do something was a guarantee that she would do it. I had to strike the right tone, find the magic words or the perfect distraction. I pulled out a stool from the breakfast bar and sat down. Maybe if I quit moving she would slow down and talk to me. *"Why start*

a fight or an argument or even a discussion with people who you know are not going to react well?" I grabbed the belt on her motorcycle jacket and pulled her toward me. I spread my legs apart and pulled her close to me. She fit right there, in my heart and between my legs and I held her close and pleaded with her not to be pushed into some action. "And who cares if they think they win or not. You win. You win because you get to live your life with me and we live in a time and place where we can be married and be out and proud and safe even in South Carolina." I slid my hands under her jacket and ran them up and down her back in what I hoped was a soothing fashion. "Why throw away that safety, why tempt fate by seeking a confrontation?"

Kelly pulled away from me and turned toward the door. "I'll think about it," she called over her shoulder as she left. I could only watch her leave and hope she would.

And with that the conversation was over. Although that was far from the last time I would discuss the issue, it was the last time I would discuss it with her. The next time it came up in conversation was when there was a mid-morning knock on the front door of our house.

Since I was working the night shift that week, the sharp rapping on the door woke me from a sound sleep. As I wandered toward the door, wiping the sleep from my eyes, I never would have imagined that my life would soon have another before and after. I had a lot of them, before and after I came out, got my job, got married . . . now there was a new one, before and after I answered that knock.

It was a tall, lean woman in a police uniform who asked my name and if I was Carrie McCallister, the next of kin of my Kelly. I wasn't quite awake enough to be afraid so I answered with a simple yes. The officer told me that there had been an incident and my wife was in the hospital. She didn't know anything more about her condition but that evidently she had been assaulted at the 7-11.

Assaulted? No, she had been systematically beaten to within an inch of her life. She was suffering from too many injuries to name them all. Kelly was in a coma. I didn't know when or if she was coming back to me. The officer took me to the hospital, which I didn't know then would become my second home. We had another discussion about the men who might have assaulted her. Kelly had snapped a picture of the vehicle the men who bothered her before were driving. I had no way of proving these were the same guys. I forwarded the picture to the police and I guess they spent a lot of time interviewing witnesses.

As I looked down at Kelly in the hospital bed I could hardly believe it was her and I was here. She didn't look like herself. There was a slackness to her face and she was way too still. Even in her sleep Kelly had moved around as if she resented having to be still. Now she was too still, just the rhythmic rise and fall of her chest and the whoosh of the machine filling and emptying her lungs for her.

She had been here, in this state for three

days. The hospital room was that sickly industrial beige that seemed to soak up all the pain of previous occupants and reflect it back at me. There were balloons, flowers, and cards on every available space. Our friends had been by to visit and let me know that if I needed anything they were there for me. The only thing I needed was Kelly to wake up and put her arms around me and my friends couldn't give me that. I was still holding out hope that the medical profession could.

I SAT IN the uncomfortable chair next to the hospital bed that had been my bed for the past three nights. I obsessively looked at her face, trying to detect a facial movement that would indicate to me that Kelly was still there. I brushed her hair back from her brow. She always had that one stubborn cowlick that was almost a curl and refused to stay where she wanted it, no matter how much product she used to try and tame it.

I whispered to her the same rhyme her father had told her when she was small. "There was a little girl, who had a little curl, right in the middle of her forehead, and when she was good, she was very, very good, and when she was bad she was horrid." I was hoping that hearing those familiar and teasing words would bring her back to me. But it didn't. Just the whoosh of the machine in time with the rise and fall of her chest.

There was a sharp rap at the hospital door that drew me out of my reverie. It was an overweight man in a too small sport coat. Everything about him screamed cop to me, from his black shoes that could use a good polish to his gray crew cut.

"Are you Carrie McCallister?"

"Yes, and you are?"

Ma'am, my name is Detective Callahan, I have a few questions for you. I need you to come downtown with me."

"Can't we just do it in the waiting room? I really don't want to leave her."

"No, ma'am, we really need to do this downtown."

"Okay, do you have someone in custody or something?"

"Something like that. Now if you will just come with me."

Alarm bells were going off. He displayed none of the professional and distant sympathy of the first officer I had dealt with. I thought maybe that was because she was a uniformed officer and he was a detective. He reached for my arm as if to pull me out of the room.

I held up my hand. "Just a minute, I need to tell her I'm leaving. I don't know if she can hear me but I need to tell her." I pushed that curl back again and whispered, "I love you, baby. I need to go downtown and help the police catch the guys that did this to you. I'll be back soon."

I heard a cough, or was it a snort from the detective. I hoped it wasn't because he was some kind of homophobe.

We got downtown and the first thing Detective Callahan did was slide a piece of paper across the table and tell me that before he asked me any questions it was standard procedure to read me my rights and I needed to sign a paper indicating that I had been given a Miranda warning. He recited the formal words that everyone who ever watched a police drama was familiar with and handed me a pen.

"Why are you reading me my rights? Aren't those only for people who are suspected of committing a crime and are in custody? Should I contact a lawyer?"

"Ma'am, you can contact a lawyer if you want but I should tell you that when people lawyer up rather than help us try and catch the person who injured their 'friend' then that . . ."

"She's not a friend, she's my wife," I retorted.

"Yes, well, I am sure you know the 'spouse' is always the first suspect when something like this happens, so we need to clear you as a suspect before we begin looking for someone else. And before we can clear you we have to give you your Miranda rights. So you want to sign this paper or you want to delay the investigation? I have plenty of cases to work." His chair screeched as he slid it back across the industrial tile in the interview room.

I could hear the quotes around his words every time he referred to Kelly as my spouse or wife. Clearly he was not a supporter of gay marriage.

I looked at the table and saw eye bolts mounted on my side. In a flash I knew they were to restrain criminals, keep them chained down during questioning. I didn't have any cuffs on but I didn't feel as though I could leave. I was torn. I really wanted to get back to Kelly in the hospital, what if she woke up and I wasn't there, or what if she . . . no I wasn't even going to think about that. "Okay, I will answer your questions and sign the paper." I picked up the pen, carefully signed, and dated the bottom and slid the paper back across the table to Detective Callahan.

"Great, let me file this away and I will be right back."

I heard the lock turn after he left the room and couldn't shake the feeling of impending doom. I didn't have my watch on so I wasn't sure how long I sat there waiting for him. I was sure I was being videotaped, like the police thought I would start talking to myself about my successful plan to have my wife attacked.

The room was freezing. After I had been alone for a few minutes it seemed to get colder. I was sure this was just part of their psychological warfare, designed to put me in a more compliant mood. It only served to make me mad. I was pushing back my chair, prepared to demand to be taken back to the hospital when I heard the lock turn and the door pushed in.

Detective Callahan and another man appeared and sat down across from me. He didn't say his name and I didn't ask. The longer I was away from the hospital the more concerned and anxious I became. "Okay, sorry about the delay but the Department floats on a sea of paperwork and all of it has to be in triplicate with copies filed in the proper place. Alright, just a few questions and we can get you out of here."

"How long is this going to take? I really want to get back to my wife." I used the term wife rather than her name because I knew he was uncomfortable with it and I wanted to drive his prejudice home.

"Well, that depends on you, ma'am," Detective Callahan replied. "Are you aware that you are the sole beneficiary of a quarter of a million dollar life insurance policy that Kelly carries?"

"Of course I am aware, she is the beneficiary of my policy as well. It is a policy that is provided through her work. What does that have to do with . . . ?" The proverbial light bulb went off. If I was a cartoon character it would have lit up the whole room. "You think I had something to do with this, don't you? That's why you left me here so long. You were getting a warrant to pull our financial records. What the fuck? How is this finding the people who attacked my wife?"

"We are doing the questioning here, not you. Now, it appears that you made a substantial cash withdrawal from your joint account a few weeks ago. Want to tell me what you needed three thousand dollars for? "

"It was to give to a friend for a deposit on our vacation rental for the summer. A bunch of us share a rental cabin at the lake for the summer and she wanted cash so I . . ."

"I'll need the name of that 'friend' if there is such a person."

"I want a lawyer." With that I felt like I had fallen down the rabbit hole and was in another world, a world I understood about as well as Alice understood Wonderland. I stood up so fast that the metal chair I was sitting in tipped over and crashed to the floor.

The detectives silently opened the door and

led me out. I guess I should have been relieved that they didn't put me under arrest but I still couldn't believe that they were looking at me. My wife was in a coma in the hospital and the police were running around trying to link the crime to me. A silent young uniformed officer took me back to the hospital where Kelly's condition remained unchanged.

THE NEXT DAY I'd gone to the store where Kelly stopped for coffee. I scoured the area around before I exited my truck to cross the trash-strewn parking lot. I entered the store and couldn't help but notice the desolate-looking coffee station.

Kelly had a weakness for 7-11 coffee. She didn't like the trendy upscale stores with snooty baristas. She liked simple strong black coffee. She always said that it shouldn't take so many words to order coffee, just small, medium, or large and black or cream and sugar. I remember her railing against Starbucks saying only in America where the majority of people only spoke one language, English, could a business get away with calling a twenty-four ounce coffee twenty in Italian. On the rare Sunday we didn't have plans I would get up before her and run down to pick up coffee and the paper. I loved to sit in bed doing the Sunday crossword while she slowly woke up as the caffeine kicked in.

The coffee counter at 7-11 was truly unpretentious and blue collar. The counter contained twelve different large urns of coffee, most of them empty at eleven a.m. on a Thursday. Kelly liked 7-11 because the coffee was inexpensive and

Women of the Year

always fresh and hot. She didn't have to talk to some kid in an apron who would spell her name wrong and screw up her order. She just strolled in, filled her own cup, laid down a couple of bucks and she was off.

Also, the 7-11 was prime people watching. They had a small selection of all kinds of grocery items, usually at three times the price you pay in a grocery store. She once asked me why people would buy food there, why they would overpay for basic necessities. My response was that there weren't that many grocery stores in the inner city so the 7-11s and other bodegas had a monopoly. If you didn't have a car you had to get your food close to home and sometimes that meant overpaying.

I think she looked at the people buying milk and cereal differently after that conversation. It wouldn't surprise me at all if she had actually paid for some stranger's milk or formula. That's the kind of woman she was, she looked tough and butch and hard as nails but she was sensitive and kind.

The packets of sugar and artificial sweetener were near a recessed cooler that held quarts of creamer. All of the containers were tipped over indicating they were empty, used up, kinda like I felt inside. Three cops stood by the nearly empty doughnut case.

I crumpled up the paper cup I had picked up and stomped over to the three men. They were talking about the football game last night. Like that was the most important thing in the world. Like catching the bastards who beat my wife was no big deal. I tensed up. I could feel the fight or flight chemicals flooding my system.

Goddammit my wife was assaulted here three days ago and they were casually discussing a wife-beating professional athlete instead of solving that crime. I wanted to yell, scream, beg, cry, make a deal with the devil, anything to get Kelly to wake up. Instead I just turned and left to go back to the hospital.

As I walked in the room I called out a cheerful, "Hey, baby," well as cheerful as I could make it. We were in day four since Kelly had been hooked up to the machines. I sat down in the chair by the bed and brushed the curl back from her forehead.

I started telling her about my day, not that there was much to say. I didn't want to tell her about the police and their accusation because I sensed that if she could hear me she would be upset. She always tried to protect me from unpleasantness and discomfort. Not that I needed protecting, I was capable of taking care of myself but that was one of those things she would do to show that she loved me. She always wanted me to be comfortable. I caught myself before I cried again. You would think that my tear ducts would be empty by now.

A young woman in a business suit came into the room. "Ms. McCallister?"

"Yes, that's me. What do you need?"

"Well, I know the doctors have been in to discuss your wife's condition with you and I wanted to speak to you about organ donation."

"Wait, what? What the fuck are you talking about?"

Women of the Year 99

"Um." She shifted uncomfortably. "Didn't the doctor speak to you this morning?"

"No, I just got here three minutes ago. What are you talking about?"

"That's okay, Ms. McCallister, I'll come back later." She turned and fled from the room.

Before I could even process what that was all about, Kelly's doctor came in trailed by a gaggle of interns. August was not a good time to be in a teaching hospital because the newly graduated doctors had just begun their internship the prior month so it felt like there was more teaching than treating going on.

Kelly's doctor ignored me and turned to the trailing interns. "Who wants to report on Ms. McCallister's condition?"

"Thirty-five-year-old female, admitted four days ago after suffering severe trauma," one of the interns said. "There are no signs of brain function returning as there have been no active spontaneous respirations after ventilator cessation. This has been confirmed with an EEG which showed electrocerebral silence. We are keeping her brain alive until we can contact the next of kin about organ donation."

"What the fuck are you talking about? I am the next of kin and no one has said anything to me about any of this."

Just then Kelly's mom walked in and stared me down like I was some sort of specimen under a microscope. "Well, since the police suspect you are behind all this, I have filed guardianship papers with the court to get power of attorney over all her medical and financial affairs. Oh, and I also filed a restraining order to have you kept away from her. There is no telling what you will do next since your plan to have someone kill her didn't work."

"You can't do this, I am her wife. We were legally married in Washington, DC last year. I have the right to make health care decisions. And what do you mean financial? All our accounts are joint accounts."

"Yes and I petitioned to have them all frozen before you move the money, you conniving little bitch. Doctor, please call security and have this . . . person removed from the hospital."

"You can't do that, I have a marriage license . . ."

"Not recognized in this state," her mother interrupted.

"Thanks to the Supreme Court it is recognized in all fifty states now. I also have a durable power of attorney that appoints me to make medical and financial decisions."

"I am going to have all that thrown out in court, we do know a few people in the legal system here South Carolina. You know they don't like your kind down here."

As a security guard entered the room to remove me per the request of Kelly's mom, I reached the end of my rope. I leaned over and kissed Kelly's cheek, told her I would be back soon and that I loved her and left the room. I went home and contacted a local attorney who had some experience in gay and lesbian rights. I was going to need someone to take up my fight both in the criminal process and the civil process. I had no idea how I was going to afford all this, particularly if the threat to freeze our joint accounts came to fruition.

As it turned out, the firm I contacted could not have been more helpful. First, my attorney, Laurie Murphy, handled the civil side of things. My accounts were not frozen and the marriage license and durable power of attorney were enough to get the interference of Kelly's mom handled. I think my attorney dropped the name Terry Schiavo more than once to remind the judge that he didn't want the attention that Jeb and George got that situation dragged on for almost fifteen years. It took a few weeks for Laurie to get me back into the hospital with Kelly. But once I was in there I wondered why I had fought so hard. It had been hard to be away from Kelly but the body in the bed was not her.

Laurie also got the criminal charges dismissed. The cops could always refile them if they came across any evidence implicating me but I got the feeling that they were done with this case. To them it was just another dyke who probably deserved what she got. I knew they wouldn't find anything else to implicate me and I doubted they would even look for anyone else.

As I sat there catching her up on where I had been the past few weeks, a clipboard invaded my space. An officious-looking woman asked if I was ready to sign the organ donation papers yet. I had met with the doctors and I knew that Kelly was not coming back. If her life could serve a purpose of making someone else not suffer the loss that I was suffering, she would want that. So I signed the papers and the nurse came in.

My friends ask me why? Why do I think someone attacked Kelly?

I. Don't. Care.

There is no reason, excuse, or rationalization that could justify to me or hopefully any court or jury of their peers any of the deliberate, systematic, and brutal beating of my wife.

I looked around the room one last time. The balloons were beginning to deflate and the flowers wilting. The cheery get well wishes no longer seemed to fit in this room where I sat, knowing that she was not going to get well, in fact, in a few short moments it would be over.

I brushed her hair back one more time, kissed her forehead, and told her I loved her even though I knew she was beyond hearing.

If they ever manage to catch the people or person who did this, will I go to the trial? No.

I have no interest in seeing the wheels of justice grind with reference to the perpetrators. They will get what they deserve or they won't. And the fact that they had a terrible childhood, or a good one or that they were beaten or that they were spoiled or any other fucking thing in the world just didn't matter. I couldn't bear to look at them and listen to whatever self-serving crap spewed out of their mouths.

I. Don't. Care.

I softly touched Kelly's cool brow as the beeps grew slower and slower until they stopped altogether. I swept the curl back off her forehead for the last time. The room was silent. All the machines had been turned off. There was no beep or whoosh keeping her alive. My life, my love slipped quietly into the night. All because she wouldn't go somewhere else for a cup of coffee and some asshat couldn't stand someone who didn't fit his little box.

September

DBAP

I CURSED UNDER my breath as I puffed my way along the nature trail in the county park. Being the sheriff of the county meant that I had to investigate all the crimes in my jurisdiction. Mostly we were a slow-moving rural area and I was only called out for minor things like kids vandalizing mailboxes and such.

There had been an uptick in criminal activity when decongestants were readily available and some idiot got the bright idea to run a meth lab in his car because he figured he could escape with his product if he ever got caught. He underestimated the flammability of his illegally manufactured goods and after lighting a cigarette in his car the resulting explosion was heard for miles. The volunteer fire department did most of the work on that one and the state forensics lab identified the cause of the fire so my role was mostly limited to interviews about the dangers of drugs. When I said uptick in serious criminal activity, what I really meant was one serious crime. Like I said, we were a slow-moving rural community. Most everyone that wanted to be a sheriff wanted to preside over an area of the country that had a bit more in the way of action (and paycheck but that was a different story).

I came into this job lean and hungry, ready to put away all the bad guys and stand up for the downtrodden. After twenty years, I was seldom surprised with any of the calls I got. However this September early morning call was the sixth reported dead body in my area in the last week. Notice I said sixth reported dead body, none of them were actual dead bodies, just reports. They all turned out to be false alarms. Ever since that anthropology professor in Kansas had begun producing her series of PSAs about DBAPS . . . you have seen those, right?

Okay. Well, let me explain. She'd go on long runs through places that she believed would be good places for a murderer to dump a dead body. She'd film herself. Well, I guess she has a crew that does the filming now, but she'd point to a pile of brush, for example, and say that would be a great place for a murderer to stash a dead body. She'd go over and examine the brush. Of course there wasn't a dead body in sight but she'd explain what you should do if there was a dead body there. She'd review what she called her DBAP or Dead Body Action Plan. I think it's a four step process—gasp, step back carefully in your own steps to preserve the evidence, call 911, and keep on-lookers away.

It was actually pretty good advice as far as preserving the scene. I didn't have a problem with the advice itself. But ever since the Logo network began airing these PSAs last week, people were seeing dead bodies everywhere.

For example, today, I was in the County Park on the hiking trail. The loop was five miles long and of course the alleged dead body was at the farthest point. No vehicles were allowed back here so I had to walk in to check out the latest report. Now, even though my job was a physical one, since I took over as Chief I did less walking and working and more sitting and talking. As a result I've developed what could kindly be known as a pooch belly. Okay, a gut that lapped over my gun belt and stretched my uniform shirt out to near the button popping stage. I could have bought some larger shirts, which would have been the smart and comfortable thing to do. But I kept telling myself that I would start working out again tomorrow. That's the thing about tomorrow, it's always a day away. (Yes, I know that's from a musical, *Annie* to be precise, so sue me, the big tough cop loves musical theatre). In any event, while tomorrow never came, my waistline kept expanding and I was really out of shape.

I was only just realizing how out of shape I was as I hoofed it around the walking trail, carrying a crime scene kit. I was huffing and puffing like the big bad wolf outside of a house of twigs. As I neared the part of the trail where the alleged dead body had been spotted I stopped, set the case down, and put my hands on my knees for a few minutes trying to catch my breath. It wouldn't do to have the sheriff show up panting like a dog in the summer sun.

I picked up the case and rounded the last curve. A younger woman in the brightest neon yellow running shorts and orange sneakers I had ever seen waved me on saying, "Nothing to see here, nope, no dead bodies, just move along. Oh, it's you, Sheriff. Glad you're here. I think it's a real live dead, um, it's a real dead body this time, I just know it."

"Oh really, are you sure this time, Helen?" Helen had reported four of the six alleged dead bodies so I was understandably a little skeptical.

"Pretty sure. I was just running along the trail here when I noticed that the edge of the trail has a pretty steep drop off. I got to thinking that it would be a great place to dump a body because mostly people don't get close enough to the edge to look over, so I stopped and looked and saw a bare leg sticking out of those brambles at the bottom of the drop off. I didn't go down there because I didn't want to destroy any evidence." She was getting excited now and speaking really fast and kind of hopping back and forth.

"Slow down, Helen. So you looked over the edge, saw what appeared to be a leg and called 911?"

Well, no, first I backed away from the edge, stepping in my own footprints so I wouldn't further destroy any evidence. Then I looked to see if there were any marks or anything at the top that would show someone had carried or pushed a body down the slope."

"Where did this happen?"

"Just up the path a little ways. I put some DBAP tape out to protect the scene and have been keeping an eye out so I could keep any bystanders away."

I walked a little further around the curve in the trail and noticed some stakes with neon purple tape stretched across the trail in two different places. The tape had DBAP alternated with Move Along and Nothing to See Here printed every six inches. "What the Sam Hill is that tape?"

"Oh, that's part of my DBAP kit. I carry it with me in this fanny pack every time I run. It has the tape, collapsible stakes, and other stuff that might be needed to preserve the scene of a dead body, or really any other crime. It's produced by Moran-Tek," Helen replied. "Dead center between the two DBAP tapes on the left is where the body is located."

I examined the trail to see if there were any marks that looked like something had been dragged along the ground. I didn't expect to see any and I didn't. There were tons of places to dump a dead body that did not involve a two-and-a-half mile hike hauling said body. I took a few pictures with the camera from my kit.

"Ooh, a camera, what a great idea. I think I will add one to my kit," Helen said from right behind me.

I jumped at the sound of her voice. I thought she was still on the other side of the tape. "Jeez, don't sneak up on me. Can you wait over there?" I pointed to the other side of the tape.

"I thought you would want me to point out the body, I'm really sure it's a body this time too."

"Okay, just stay behind me and step in my footprints."

We both carefully walked up to the edge and peered over the side. Holy Mother of Cotton, it was a body. Or at least it looked like one, or did it? I pulled the binoculars out of my kit to get a better view of what looked like a leg ten feet down the ravine. My mind was racing and I thought about extracting the body, preserving the evidence, identifying the victim, and all the sudden I put the binoculars down and turned to Helen. "Sorry, darling, it's another false alarm. That appears to be the mannequin missing from the sporting goods store. You can tell by the angle of the foot and the line for the joint to articulate when showing off various types of sporting footwear."

"Damn, Sheriff, I thought we had one this time. Oh well, see you later." Helen turned and grabbed her DBAP tape and collapsible stakes and stuffed them back in her fanny pack. "Maybe next time."

I put all my stuff back in my kit and huffed and puffed back down the trail. The car was only two-and-a-half miles away. Hmmm, almost made me wonder if Helen was in cahoots with my wife to make sure I was getting more exercise.

October

Companion

"IT'S WAY PAST time, Jessie," my bestie Salem said.

It was true but that didn't mean I wanted to accept it. Salem and I sat eating breakfast at our favorite local farm-to-table restaurant Eggsistential.

"I know you think so, but it's only been a year since she left me." I twisted my ring, a nervous habit that manifested itself over the past year and a half.

"It's been closer to two years but who's counting. Okay, I am counting and I can't stand to see you moping around anymore. I get that Kelsey was special. She will always have a special place in your heart but you need to close that chapter and move on. There's another one out there for you." Salem got the attention of the waitress by waving her coffee cup in the air. Our server stopped by with a pot of coffee to fill our cups on the way to take the order from the table next to us. The clatter of silverware against the heavy china plates provided a steady background to our conversation. Eggistential was always busy but weekday mornings were a mad rush as customers would stop in to get a quick bite on the way to the office. I had chosen this restaurant in the hopes that the atmosphere would get me out of having this type of personal conversation. It appeared my hopes were in vain.

I picked up a piece of bacon and dipped it in the maple syrup. Don't judge me until you try it. "Look, it's not like she could be replaced. After all, when Kelsey departed, she left behind a heart-sized hole in my chest that had only just begun to scar over." I eyed the rest of Salem's bacon across the table. "You are right; I don't think I can live the rest of my life without some companionship."

Maybe it was time to find another, even if the new girl could not fill Kelsey's place in my heart. I was going to do things differently this time. With Kelsey, it had just happened. I wasn't looking but she wormed her way into my heart somehow. This time it was going to be different. I was going to establish firm rules. The new girl would know her place and keep to it. I needed the company but I couldn't, no wouldn't, put my heart at risk again.

We finished up breakfast and I headed to the office.

I moved through the reception area, nodding to the receptionist. My P.A., well one of them, hurried over, fumbling with her files.

"Miss Foster, I moved your two o'clock as requested and your conference call will be ready in a few minutes."

I took the file and handed the jacket to her. I loved making the opposition squirm. The P.A placed a coffee on my desk and I relaxed into the chair, checking through my crammed inbox. I'd cleared most of it from home before I met Salem for breakfast. It didn't matter how fast I deleted an e-mail, another always appeared and they

Women of the Year

seemed to multiply when left unattended for too long.

I cocked my head. Wouldn't you know it, an e-mail addressing my concern. Instead of the usual ways I was going to try a new service. One that promised that, for the right price, I could have everything I was looking for in my new "friend."

The conference call was long and painful for the opposition. That's what happened when any soon-to-be-ex spouse of my client tried to hide assets during the discovery process. I was going to squeeze every cent out of him and he knew it. While he protested, I began working on a list of non-negotiable qualities that was part of a questionnaire designed to assist me in narrowing down my choices.

Obviously female. Except for my father there had never been any men in my life. I double-checked the website and smiled. This group was not like e-Harmony which only matched men with women and women with men!

"I can do, say, a fifty-fifty split. That's more than fair, after all she isn't entitled to all of it," the other attorney offered. Always the case with a new one. I had never been up against him in a divorce case but he would learn.

"Eighty-twenty to my client. She might not have been entitled to it but your guy tried to hide it, tried to cheat his wife out of all the money." Okay, gender decided, what next? Ah yes, age. Well, I was certainly not interested in really young. Frankly I didn't have the energy to keep up with a youngster.

"Now, Miss Foster, we don't need to—"

"Eighty five-fifteen." Kelsey was fairly young when we met and I was not interested in going through the drama associated with someone that age again.

"There's no way we can meet that figure."

"Ninety-ten." By the same token I didn't want someone too old to enjoy the things I liked doing outdoors, such as hiking the trails in the nearby national park and picnics in the park with friends. Not too old, not too young. That wasn't very specific but hopefully that would give me a wider range of choices.

"Okay, I can do eighty-twenty but only on the 'newly located' assets," he said, sounding like he was hiding under his desk.

"Done." My client had only expected the fifty-fifty split. I always got the extra. That was why I commanded such high fees.

I moved through the rest of the list without much thought as he scrambled to keep hold of his client's property. Color was unimportant; I didn't care if her hair was long or short. She had to be able to handle being around cats, dogs, and kids as many of my friends had some or all. I finished up the questionnaire the same time as the call and e-mailed it off.

About a month later, my client had more than she could have dreamed of. I took her call, enjoying the delight in her voice. I clicked through my e-mails as she gushed.

As an e-mail caught my attention and I sat forward. My application had been accepted and the organization was sponsoring a get together.

It was just a meet and greet for their paying clients like me to encounter their matches and see if there was potential there.

"I even got the boat . . ." She carried on but my heart clenched. I wasn't sure I was ready. It had only been two years. Was that long enough? Could I look at the new girl without thinking of Kelsey? What if I called her by Kelsey's name? Was it too long? Had I been on my own so long that she wouldn't be able to fit into my new post-Kelsey life? Did the fact that I was still defining my life as before and after Kelsey mean I wasn't ready?

"Miss Foster, are you still there?"

I blinked a few times. "Yes, yes, I'm still here." Questions flickered through my mind. I hovered over delete.

"I recommended you to my colleague. She . . ." I accepted the invitation, heard the mention of a potential client, and turned my attention back to work.

The event was being held on October 11, National Coming Out Day. Usually my group of friends would get together and tell coming out stories over cocktails on this day. The more we drank the more far-fetched the stories became. That didn't mean they weren't true, it just meant that our whole group led fairly open and out lives. Since we were an open and gregarious bunch, we almost always had a new coming out story to tell every year. Sometimes it was coming out to the baker when ordering an anniversary cake, sometimes it was an innocent question from a new co-worker and sometimes it was a front page picture at a marriage equality rally. But not this year. I was skipping it for what I hoped would be a good reason.

As I drove out to my place, my thoughts drifted back to Kelsey and why it hadn't worked. One of the things that I had put on my list was that I demanded certain standards of behavior. In order to make sure that happened I required my future companion undergo some basic training prior meeting her. Nothing too outré but when we were in a room together I wanted to ensure that all her attention was focused on me. It sounded a bit off the wall but I needed to control this relationship much more than my relationship with Kelsey.

I stopped at a red light, ignoring the admiring look from the guy in the car next to me. I really needed to have the new girl obey me and follow some basic and simple rules. I was doing this to protect myself. I couldn't fall into this relationship as deeply as I had the last one. I just couldn't. If the new one ended like the old one, I don't know that I could survive.

I fiddled with my ring again, eased my foot down, and left the guy trailing. If I was able to make it clear from the beginning that I was in charge, maybe I would be able to maintain enough distance to protect my heart. Kelsey and I had on-going struggles about who was in charge. She seemed to think that she could do whatever she wanted regardless of my disapproval.

I hit the button to open the electric gates at my house. I had spoiled her so perhaps I was to blame for some of her behavior. It's not that she'd been bad, not exactly. She had occasionally done things that she knew I didn't want her to do.

I headed in through the front door. A picture of her still taunted me. I picked it up and ran my thumb over her face. When she inevitably got caught, I didn't always follow through with the discipline I had threatened. I'm pretty sure that led her to try and get away with more and more unacceptable behaviors.

I sighed and put the picture down. It was why I wanted someone who knew her place and why I had contracted with this particular organization. Their reputation for turning out obedient matches was unrivaled.

When October 11th rolled around I still wasn't sure I could go through with it. The protocol was an initial meet and greet with some semi-private "getting to know you" time. It was really just an opportunity to see if there was enough there to warrant taking the next step.

Each day, I read and re-read through the e-mail. It was all pretty highly regulated. I understood the necessity of this. They needed to make sure that the—let's call them candidates—were safe and protected. Customers, like myself, were paying a premium amount for the service. We trusted that the organization had made sure that all the candidates were healthy, disease free, and socialized to requested standards of each individual customer.

When it was time to get ready, I pulled out a suit, then put it back. No, too formal. I pulled out my favorite sweater then put that back too. No, too casual. I wanted to be comfortable but casual. I didn't want to look like I'd tried too hard . . .

I needed just the right mix of dominant but not aggressive, playful but not easy, fun but not a pushover. I decided on freshly laundered khakis and a scoop-necked t-shirt with a collared shirt over it. Perfect.

I entered the event and glowered at the guy on the door as he scoured the list before finding my name.

"Miss Foster, please go right on in. Kendra will be with you shortly."

The event was not open to the public and the participants had paid a premium to be here so the security was pretty tight to keep the riff raff out.

A buxom redhead with an infectious smile tottered over to me. "Hi, Jessie, can I call you Jessie? My name is Kendra and I'll be showing you around this evening."

I opened my mouth. "I pre—"

"Good. Now you'll meet all your girls in a private room." She waved to the man who was sitting with a coffee cup in front of him. His cup looked untouched as he eyed the door. "You walk by and take a look. If you like what you see then you can go in with supervision. There's no pressure. If you don't like how she looks or anything at all, you don't have to go in."

"What about other clients?" There were a few more clients loitering around the coffee machine.

"We just want to focus on you for right now. Don't worry about anyone else. Let's just get in there and find you a match shall we?" The woman ushered me toward a hallway.

I looked down the hall and noticed several doors and a couple more hallways. A few other people were being ushered about by clipboard carrying representatives of the service.

"Now, all your matches are in the first four doors on the left. I suggest just strolling by and glancing in at each girl on the first pass. That will give you a feeling of the type of matches we have selected for you." Kendra took my arm and led me down the hall.

"So do I get to go in and meet them all?"

"I think just walk by first and then you can go in and spend some time with any of the candidates that strike your fancy. Be aware that the rooms are monitored."

I rolled my eyes. I was not going to engage in anything untoward, not here in what was practically public space. "I understand."

"No pressure, spend as much or as little time with the candidates as you want. One more thing, there may be other clients here who have been matched with some of the same candidates as you." Kendra tapped at her clipboard. "There is nothing worse than feeling that soul-to-soul connection with one of your candidates only to find out later that she was selected by another customer." She flashed me a smile. "We operate on a first claimed basis. So, if you make a decision, let me know immediately and I will mark your choice as unavailable to anyone else right way."

We walked down the hallway and she paused for a moment. "Are you ready?"

I nodded. My heart, aching for Kelsey, pounded with the hope that I could find the right match. I took a breath. No, this was about setting the tone. I was in charge, that had to be clear. I straightened my shoulders and drew myself up to my full height.

I strode by, looking into the rooms. Each match was standing up, looking at the doorway as I walked by. I just glanced in, made eye contact, nodded at each candidate, and continued on. The first three were all blonde. Not that it was a preference but I wasn't complaining. There was nothing that would cause me to reject any of them out of hand but I didn't feel . . . like I had with Kelsey.

I sighed. This was a stupid idea, what chance did the others have of making me feel like she had? I glanced at the exit.

"Jessie, I think you might like this next one," Kendra said with a knowing smile.

I could only manage a nod and followed her to the final door. I took a breath and peered in. The blonde inside turned. Our eyes met and there was almost an audible click as a piece of my soul seemed to be restored. The piece that had been missing for two years, since Kelsey.

I slammed shut my eyes. I couldn't believe I was doing this. I was never one for impulsive decisions. I made lists and carefully considered the pros and cons before making decisions like this.

I nodded to Kendra, trying to ignore her confident smile. I seemed to be watching someone else inhabiting my body "I'll take her and I want her to come home with me tonight."

"That would be highly irregular," said Kendra said even though she was already filling out the form on her clipboard. "I am not sure . . ."

Business as usual for her. I knew the look and the charming smile well. I often used it just before I handed my bill over. "I understand there may some additional charges associated with this and that's fine. Just let me know that you can make this happen." I fixed her with the kind of stare I did my opponents across the bargaining table. "Mark her off as unavailable. Work out the details and come get me when the two of us can leave. I'll be in there getting to know her better while you are taking care of all that." With that I turned, dismissing Kendra, and entered the room focused on my future.

As we made our way to the exit, Kendra hurried over, a large smile on her face. She handed me the completed paperwork.

"You know, she's never been separated from her sister in the six months they've been here. I know they're close." She was good. I could have used her in my firm with that kind of delivery, low key, but used to getting people to buy whatever she was selling. "You wouldn't be interested in twins would you?"

I sighed and looked at down at my girl. Her big soft eyes looked hopefully into mine. How could I say no?

"Okay," I said, leaning down to ruffle her blonde locks. "How much more trouble could two golden retrievers be than one?"

November

I See You

I COULDN'T BELIEVE Thanksgiving was here again already. It seemed like way less than a year ago I was forced to go through the day long festivities of conspicuous consumption, football, and the political lamentations of a crowd to the right of Genghis Khan. It was the Wednesday before Thanksgiving and that was the one holiday my mother demanded that I show up for. I'm not sure why I continued to go. What could she really do to me? I mean we didn't talk on the phone, we were not involved in each other's lives, she absolutely refused to accept that I was a lesbian but still . . . every year I went and every year I returned home wishing I had a family that I was close to and, most importantly, one that accepted me.

Maybe one year I would have reason to not go, a family of my own that I wanted to give thanks for and spend time with. If I ever did have that I would not subject her to my family and their ambivalence toward me, an ambivalence that bordered on hostility. I would go to the house I grew up in but I would not go quietly.

I STOOD BEFORE the mirror in the hotel room and checked my appearance. For a forty something year old I thought I looked pretty good. I looked at myself, trying to imagine how a potential date might see me. I touched my short spiked hair and let out another sigh. It seemed that additional greys had shown up overnight. I was hoping that it was just the light in the hotel room or, alternatively that the lights in the bar wouldn't highlight this all too obvious sign of my increasing age.

I turned around to see how the view looked from the back. My tattered Levi's fit me like a second skin. The rips and worn places gave a strategic glimpse of my tan skin. Worn but still spit shined Doc Martins and a tight T-shirt from Green Day's American Idiot tour completed the outfit. I knew Green Day was really after my time, I was much older than the majority of people at their last concert but something about their music spoke to me. They had a take no shit from anyone attitude that I so wanted to emulate in my life. Despite all the hopelessness in the lyrics to their songs, the music made me feel the exact opposite. It infused me with a desire to take action.

One last look and I was ready to head out the door. I was the quintessential butch in an era where more and more of the kids of this generation eschewed labels like butch and femme, or any labels at all. I almost seemed to be invisible when I went out to the bar these days.

I PICKED UP the room key and my phone from the dresser, ignoring the message from my mother. I needed space. There was only so much time I could invest in dealing with the hostilities or even worse, the lack of interest of my family.

I was headed out to the bar for a little dancing, drinking, and hopefully some distraction!

I gave the cabdriver the address and he turned around and looked at me as if to ask did I really wanted to go to that neighborhood?

"Are you sure you got the right address, lady?"

I told him the address again. He looked me up and down for a second and sighed a long heavy sigh.

I pushed the button to open the window and watched the streets roll past. As we sped away from the hotel district we headed toward the river. The hustle and bustle of downtown gave way to the factories and warehouses that had once been the lifeblood of this city. Now building after building was boarded up and abandoned. Every so often I heard the screech of a metal grate being lowered as the remaining businesses closed for the night. The city was dying. The auto industry that had made the city great was gasping its last breath as cheaper foreign alternatives crammed the highways. The city failed to grow and adapt to changes that had been coming since the seventies. If my hometown were a person, it would raise a querulous voice from the nursing home rocking chair, decrying the loss of an America that only ever existed on television shows from the fifties.

I wondered how long it would take to get a cab home from this abandoned neighborhood. It didn't matter. I'd wait. I knew I would be having a drink or two and I was not going to risk leaving the car there or driving after drinking.

The taxi driver pulled over. I swiped my credit

card and accepted the receipt. As I stepped out onto the cracked sidewalk the cab sped away like there was something contagious in the air. I looked down the side street and saw more of the same boarded-up row homes that had once housed working class families but were now collateral damage from the white flight to the suburbs, years of benign neglect and the general desertion of this part of town. The people who lived here now stayed out of necessity, never by choice.

I stepped toward the club and a plastic bag blew against my leg. I shook it off. An urban version of tumbleweed from Silver Star Diner. The original diner was way over the other side of town, actually pretty close to my hotel. I used to love that place. They sold the best breakfast I'd ever tasted. I wondered if I could make time to stop in. Tomorrow was family day and I was heading back home early Friday morning but I had to eat breakfast someplace and they were open twenty-four hours a day.

The hole in the wall club I was going to was called Going My Way and it was located in the worst part of town. Every city I visited was the same. The industrial deserted section that no one wanted to be seen in always housed the bars of my people.

The soot and dirt from industry coated the warehouses, cheap rooming houses, and row homes that were subdivided into inexpensive apartments. The streets were cobblestone which rattled the suspension of every vehicle that ventured down here. While the neighborhood was never what you would call bustling, the evening turned the place into a ghost town. Those who visited the bar as forgotten as the place itself . . .

Some were bold and brazen, owning this world with every step striding up to the door and flinging it open. Some scuttled in with a furtive glance over the shoulder for the prying eyes of a neighbor or a family member. Something about the impending holiday brought us all out. We needed to be there. We needed the release. A lot of people in the community had good relationships with their families or weren't out to their families but many of us had issues.

It wasn't the same for me. I was out but not accepted. I soaked in the comfort of the faded rainbow flag flapping above the door, I needed to be immersed, surrounded by lesbians. If the evening progressed and led to total immersion in one lesbian back at her place, so much the better.

I pulled open the door and was assaulted by the thrumming bass of the dance music. Its throbbing deep line filled my senses and my head bobbed to the beat. I didn't recognize the song. No surprise. I didn't really listen to the new club and techno satellite channels. I was into the throwback tunes from the late eighties when I was a club rat. I paid the cover and dove into the crowd, heading toward some liquid courage.

It was a mixed crowd; most places couldn't support a women's only bar. That was okay, for the most part we segregated ourselves, only really integrating with the boys on the dance floor.

I ghosted through the crowd, moving in the rhythm of the bar, two steps then pause for someone to slip by, another step and slide to the right. My movements were as much of a dance in this packed crowd as anything happening on the dance floor. At the bar I tried to get the attention of one of the two people fighting to keep up with the orders being fired their way. The young man, in short shorts and nothing else, ignored my waving hand. The other bartender was female wearing the shortest possible shorts that didn't quite cover her butt and a midriff bearing tank top with strategic rips in the small amount of fabric. As I stared over the bar I marveled at her ability to navigate the cramped space without running into the liquor or the other bartender or flashing the waiting crowd with a wardrobe malfunction.

I got it, the bar was hot, they were hot and they worked mostly for tips, but she carried on serving the group of twenty-something kids in the corner. Anyone over the age of thirty was invisible. I doubted she could contemplate being thirty much less stepping into her forties. Great, now I was invisible to her and my family. Community, right, well, I had something those kids didn't. I stuck out a twenty and her eyes glinted as they caught sight of the waving bill. Yeah, sometimes older meant more money but it also meant more experience in getting what I wanted.

"Two bottles of Yuengling . . . and keep the change."

She grinned, clasped the money, and grabbed my beers from the cooler with a wink. It was a sure fire way to keep her looking for me if I returned for another.

The boys occupied tables to the left of crowded dance floor. To the right was a half wall with some stools that separated two pool tables from the rest of the bar. It was less crowded.

I strolled into the pool area, noticing the average age was much higher than the outer part of the bar. I scrawled my name on the chalkboard with the shortest list. There was one board for each table. It was the same every time I went to a gay bar. The lesbians ran the pool table. When I first started playing I would usually lose. Then I met Tory who taught me all the angles, well, the ones on the pool table anyway. When I played regularly I could hold the table against all challengers. I hadn't played in a long time but I was pretty sure I still had the requisite skills.

The winner took on the next person on the list and there were five names ahead of mine so I settled in to wait. There weren't that many cues in the rack next to the chalkboards and they all appeared rather old and not very straight, hmmm, kind of like me. I laughed out loud at my thought and caught the attention of one of the players. Unfortunately, she had just missed a shot and thought I was laughing at her. She crossed the room and got up close in my personal space.

"Something funny about the way I play pool?"

"No, not at all, I just had a thought that struck me funny. Here," I said, holding out one of my beers.

She took my peace offering without so much as a thank you and stalked back to her game.

I placed my one remaining beer on the narrow

shelf, just wide enough for a drink and a pack of cigarettes, running along the length of the wall.

The woman who appeared to have been running the other table stood near me, watching her hapless opponent take another bad angle on one shot. She was wearing the typical butch outfit, jeans, a tight t-shirt, freshly shined motorcycle boots, and an attitude to match. She grinned at me when she caught me checking her out. She was not the type I usually went for, but that type had landed me single again. Something about her drew me in. Her opponent sank the eight ball and lost, shrugged, and walked away to the jeers of her nearby friends. The winner erased the name on top of the board and called out for the next player.

As she was waiting for the new player to rack the balls, I turned to grab my beer. I glanced over my shoulder and caught her checking me out. She ran her eyes up my body like a caress. I could almost feel her long fingers brush along my hip, graze my breast, and cup my cheek.

I didn't know what was the matter with me. Maybe it was hormones, maybe it was the whole Thanksgiving family interaction thing but I felt something. I couldn't stop looking at her. Not when she drank, not when she glanced my way or played pool. I was smitten in a way that was unlike me. Maybe it was the way she was looking at me, she was clearly checking me out. Maybe it as the way she commanded the table, even when she wasn't taking a shot.

And man, was she in her element. She demolished every opponent. In one game I watched her run the table, sinking all her shots without allowing her challenger so much as one.

The feeling built as I soaked every nuance of her in. The way she leaned over the table, the way her eyes scoped all the angles, her sultry voice calling the shot. As she stroked the pool cue I imagined her fingers stroking my cheek, touching me the way her eyes had been caressing me all evening.

My name was next on the list but I didn't want to play pool. When she stood up and called for next I walked over to her and stuck my hand out.

"I think I'm up, my name is . . ."

"I know your name, Sammie." She flicked out her finger toward the chalkboard and slinked one hip to the table. "Somehow I don't get the feeling pool is the game you want to play tonight." She held out the pool cue with a hungry smile.

I took the offered cue and leaned against it. "Since you seem to know so much about me, how about letting me know your name?"

She rolled her hand over the felt of the table as if she owned the place. "Everybody knows me around here. I'm Morgan."

It had been a long time since anyone had really known me. I thought Kendra had been the one for me. I had imagined the whole bit, the white picket fence, kids, dogs, and of course the happily ever after. But that had all come crashing down when I got home one night and found her half of the closet empty and a note on the table pronouncing that there was no us anymore. It had been just over a year ago, after I had gone to my family's house for Thanksgiving. I thought Kendra understood. Maybe she understood more than I did, that she was not worth bucking my mother and having our own Thanksgiving. Time had given me perspective and a measure of acceptance of my part in the break-up.

"Well, obviously I am not from around here, well not anymore." I placed my bottle to my lips to drain away the thoughts. What was the use in going back there? "I'd like to know what everybody else knows about you . . ." I caught her gaze lingering on my neck and smiled. I knew exactly how to forget. "But not here." I gestured around the crowded bar.

Morgan made a sweet humming sound, rolling the cue ball over her fingers. "Could be interesting. I'm not used to someone else making the moves." She flicked the cue ball up with her knuckles and caught it in her other hand. "I usually lead and she follows if she wants to or I find someone who does."

She popped the ball up again, I caught it. "I'm not a very good follower but I could perhaps be persuaded to take turns for the right incentive."

Morgan leaned over, cupped my hip, and pulled me closer. She put her mouth next to my ear. "What kind of persuasion?"

I turned my head. I teased at her lips with the tip of my tongue. "The kind best done horizontally and with fewer clothes."

Another benefit to getting older was not playing as many games. She took my hand and started dragging me through bar but I pulled her next to me. I might not have known where exactly we were going but we were going to get there side by side.

WE REACHED HER pickup truck. I spun around, pressed her against it, claimed her mouth with mine, demanding she yield. She shoved me off her, panting.

"Get in." She yanked open the door and strode around to the driver's side. I hopped in and just managed to close the door as she squealed out of the parking lot.

I couldn't keep my hands off her. I couldn't stop touching her, running my hands over her jeans, over her thighs. She gripped my wrist and screeched to a stop. We'd made it to a driveway. I knew this part of town. It was close to my uncle's house.

She shut off the engine and clamped hold of my wrist. "I'll pay you back for that."

I pulled my wrist hauling her toward me until her lips were inches from mine. "You were squirming around in your seat like you were enjoying it."

She jumped out of the truck and strode toward the house. I paused to admire her firm ass as she made her way across the lawn and then scrambled to catch up.

Once inside, we began what went on through the night, explosive passion fraught with the need for each of us to be in control. Sometimes temporarily yielding control but inevitably reasserting it with the next breath.

Neither of us slept much, it was more like a break in the action to renew our strength to once again conquer each other. It wasn't making love, but seemed so much more than just sex.

Wrapped up in her arms felt like more comfort than I realized I needed.

"Any reason why you were in town?" Morgan asked, trailing her finger over my arm. Her voice was heavy, like her eyelids as she gazed down at me.

"Mom, Thanksgiving meal." I sighed. "I guess I shouldn't be so mad about it. It's not like they kicked me out or disowned me." I hated that they didn't care or want to know about my heart or seem to care about my life. I was their only daughter, but I could never fully share my life with them because they couldn't accept me. "It's all so messed up."

"Yeah. I got the full bags on the street treatment. Sixteen and put out on the curb like I was trash." She flicked her gaze away. I could see the hurt glinting there still. It never vanished. It never faded. "My mistake was getting caught."

She laughed although it sounded close to a sob.

"Hey, their problem, not yours."

Morgan took a long breath. "Then I got a job and a place of my own." She dismissed it with a wave. "Old news."

I knew it wasn't as simple as she made it sound. It never is for gay kids, especially not young girls. I turned over and held her close and just let her feel me.

Why was it that the scars inflicted by parents seemed so close to the surface no matter how old the wounds? Did a kid ever stop wanting parental love and approval?

Women of the Year

The alarm pulled me out of the sex-induced coma and I groaned. I didn't want to face my family. Morgan reached up and pulled me back into her arms.

I was tempted to pick up where we had left off, I knew I couldn't. Not just because my body was sore, the good kind of well-used sore, but because I had to go expose myself to a different kind of pain. I tried to pull away but Morgan leaned close.

"I wish you could stay. I couldn't pull off a full turkey dinner but I could whip up something. Maybe we could . . ." Her voice trailed away as she watched me hurry around the room picking up my clothes.

My heart fluttered but panic also flooded through me. I didn't dare look at her. I didn't think I could deal with the hurt. Why would she care so much after just a night?

"I'll drive you." She handed me my phone and I stared down at it. I wished I had the courage to stay or ask for her number. Instead I let her drive me and said nothing. I wished for the courage to not wash her scent off but to carry the scent of her passion as a shield.

I GOT TO my parent's house in time to handle the basic kitchen tasks that experience had shown I would not screw up, like peeling potatoes, stirring the gravy, and setting the table. When I walked through the door my mom's first words were, "Would it have killed you to dress up a little bit?"

I glanced down at my freshly ironed dress

pants and button-down oxford shirt and swallowed a snarky comeback. I walked through the kitchen to hang my coat on the coatrack that stood guard near the back door. It was placed there so that kids and grandkids could kick off boots on the mud porch rather than track them through the house and hang their coats up rather than drop them anywhere. I paused, thinking of all the times I had come inside soaked after a snowball fight with my twin brother Samuel. As a faint smile lingered, my mom called from the kitchen, "Samantha Anne, these potatoes aren't going to peel themselves."

I walked toward the kitchen through the dining room, noting the scratch, really more of a gouge, in the center of the table from a game of spoons that went horribly bad when I was ten. I never could do things halfway. Back then, before I proved to be the disappointment of a lifetime to my parents, we used to gather around this very table and play games, sometime card games like Uno or dice games like Yahtzee. Often we would tell jokes that would result in stomach aches from all the laughter. As I looked around now, the only thing that remained of me in the room was that scratch in the center of the table.

The photos were all of Sam and his kids. I see that the one of his ex-wife had finally been removed. It hung there for years, presumably as my mom's commentary on divorce. Our very Catholic family had never had a divorce prior to my brother. For a brief shining moment in time it moved me out of the position of least favorite child.

I returned to begin my toil in the kitchen. Really I was pretty hopeless. My mother had been trying to get me to show an interest in cooking since I got thrown out of Home Economics class in high school but to no avail. I would rather heat up something fast in the microwave. Yeah, it didn't taste all that great but it was easy. My girlfriend, strike that ex-girlfriend, had been a good cook. We had a system, she cooked and I cleaned the kitchen. But since she dumped me, traded me in for a younger model really, I had been surviving on carry out and Lean Cuisine. Today's dinner would be a welcome change.

"Samantha, set the table."

I walked into the dining room and started unfolding the tablecloth.

"No, not that one, Samantha. Really, how many years have you been eating Thanksgiving dinner here? Use the Thanksgiving tablecloth."

My mom opened a drawer in the credenza and pulled out the tablecloth with the fall foliage on it. I just didn't pay enough attention to things like that I guess. Just one more thing for me to get wrong, one more reason I was not good enough and never would be.

"Hey, Sam, get off your ass and help me set the table," I yelled.

"Language, young lady," my mom said. "Besides, your brother is watching the kids."

"More like watching the football game," I muttered half under my breath.

"What was that?"

"Nothing, Mom."

I glanced into the living room. As I suspected,

no kids to be found. From the muffled giggles coming from the back bedroom, they were tending to themselves with the toys they kept at Grandma's house. Sam, watching the Lions play, smirked up at me from his seat in the recliner.

"Sometimes it's good to be the baby," said my two minutes younger than me brother.

"You have always been a baby but in this family it's good to be a boy," I replied.

"Both of you hush," my father said. "I'm trying to watch the game. It's almost halftime. If your mom gets dinner on the table soon I won't miss any of the game."

As my mom called to the men to come to the table my brother tried to turn the TV so they could continue watching the football game while destroying in ten minutes a meal that had taken over five hours to prepare. I walked into the living room and turned the TV off. My mother nodded approvingly and my dad shushed my brother when he began to voice his complaints.

As we bowed our heads, my father said the Thanksgiving grace. "Dear Lord, thank you for this food we are about to eat and thank you for blessing this family with enough to eat and a place to live."

My uncle tried to add on to the prayer by bringing politics into it. He started by asking for a Republican win in next year's presidential race.

"This is not MSNBC so it is not 'the place for politics,'" Sam interrupted. "Let's keep this year about our personal gratitude and leave that out of our celebration for once."

I couldn't believe my brother had said that. It felt like he was standing up for me, even though I was not the subject of discussion. Well, not overtly the subject. I was the only non-Republican at the table.

As Jim stared open mouthed at Sam I chimed in with an amen in the hopes of cutting off the prayer. Sam followed suit and my mom handed me the bowl of stuffing to begin passing around. After the first round of food had been devoured and the family took a bit of a break before diving in for round two, it started. I knew it was coming, I should have been used to it. My heart and soul should be scabbed over enough so the sideways comments and pointed remarks didn't hurt. But my heart and soul were fully functional and they hurt, no ached, from the lack of acceptance.

It started off easy. Everyone knew I was a Democrat but I stopped expressing political beliefs in my twenties. I knew I was never going to change their minds and you would think they would realize they were never going to change mine, but alas, I had to hear it at every family gathering. It was why the only holiday I attended anymore was Thanksgiving. I made excuses for the other family obligation days but missing turkey day was an unforgiveable sin. This year it began with Syrian refugees.

"We can't let them into our country because you never know . . ." Uncle Jim said.

Oh, how I wanted to respond. I had it all worked out. I was going to draw the corollary between Mary and Joseph seeking shelter to give birth to Jesus and these refugees needing the same kind of assistance. But I bit my tongue. The Jesus they all knew was a white man, probably actually American, certainly not Jewish and the witty rejoinder would have flown by them without making a dent.

But this time my father jumped in. "We are not discussing politics at the table this year. If that means we don't talk at all that's fine with me but refugees, the presidential race, heck even the mayoral race are all off limits at *my* table this year. If you don't like my rules you can leave *my* house. Are we clear?" He glared at my uncle but met the eyes of everyone sitting around the table to drive his point home.

But then they jumped from refugees and presidential candidates to gay marriage. To my family, this wasn't politics, it was religion. It was an attack on them personally because their religion disagreed. This was certainly more personal to me. Not that I ever thought I would get married, but it was nice to know that I could and my country would recognize it even while my family did not. I bit my tongue.

The next topic was repealing "Obama care" because it was going to make the country go broke because of all the entitlements "those people" were getting. That lovely quote came from Aunt Peggy who had been collecting disability checks from the government since she hurt her back and couldn't work. Funny how the back pain didn't stop her from chasing kids around all day in her unlicensed, strictly cash, day care center. Funny how entitlements were defined as what other people get, not what the government dished out to members of my family. This time it was shut down with a stern look of warning from my father.

We began passing around the bowls of food for seconds and I admit, I did get a little passive aggressive. When someone complimented me on the mashed potatoes (which I had only peeled, nothing else) I replied it wasn't hard, it's not like brain surgery . . . or being the president, which was even harder.

By this time my father had returned to his football game in the living room and the ban on politics was ignored without an enforcer. At least they all kept their voices down so he couldn't hear them from the other room. When the conversation turned to Ted Cruz and how he was going to put the Supreme Court in its place and overturn the recent decisions he disagreed with, I chimed in.

"I hope he plans to overturn the Citizens United and the Hobby Lobby decisions as well." Of course no one knew what I was talking about because they got their political opinions spoon fed to them from the talking heads on Fox news. And who cared about campaign finance and birth control when we had decisions that settled those issues once and for all. Why was it that the decisions of the Supreme Court that supported their world view were legally appropriate and settled the issue for all time but when that same court legalized gay marriage or abortion or a watered-down version of universal health care it was the over-reaching of five unelected judicial activists?

Aunt Carol started in next. "The gays ran that bakery out of business in Washington. And what about that poor Kim Davis going to jail because she didn't want to violate her religious beliefs by issuing a marriage license to some homos."

I bit my tongue but oh how I wished that someone would stand up and remind the people sitting around this table that they were not talking about "those people" they were talking about a member of the family. They were talking that way about me. But no one did. No one stopped it. It was like I wasn't even there.

Just then, I felt my pants vibrating. Well actually it was my phone that was in my pants but it served the purpose of distracting me. It was a text which simply read, "I see you and I really like what I see."

It was from Morgan. She must have added herself to my contacts when I wasn't paying attention the night before. And all of the sudden it didn't matter. My whole family could be Republican or tea party or anti-gay or anti-refugee or whatever they wanted. None of it impacted me because there was someone out there who saw me, looked past what was on the outside, and forged a connection.

I pushed my chair back and stood up, phone in hand, texting back, "Want some company? Because I see you too."

December

Honor Flight

I CHERISHED MY weekends and did not easily give them up. I worked hard during the week and spent some evenings doing volunteer work but generally weekends were sacrosanct. Putting myself through school had resulted in way too many jobs where weekend work was mandatory. I spent many a menial Saturday dreaming of sleeping in and having two full days off where my schedule was my own. I maintained that position for several years after I had a Monday through Friday job. Then I heard about Honor Flight. It's an organization that flies veterans to Washington, DC and takes them on tours of the monuments. Escorting men and women who were willing to lay their lives on the line for me, to protect my freedom and my way of life seemed like a great reason to give up one Saturday a month.

It was a bit of a grueling schedule as I would wake up at oh dark thirty to get to the airport and meet the group. I would sit with one veteran on the flight and escort him to the memorial of the war that he had served in. It was living history. The stories the veterans told me were stories of bravery and sacrifice, but it was always the bravery and sacrifice of their brothers-in-arms, not their own. Maybe that was a generational thing but these men (and on the five honor flights I had participated in, the veterans were all men) didn't consider what they did as extraordinary. They just did their duty. In the reality-TV, look-at-me, win-a-ribbon-for-showing-up world that seemed to surround me, this modesty was refreshing.

I got a call from the honor flight coordinator in late November asking if I was available December 14th. Since I was under the impression that we didn't make Honor Flights in December because of the dicey DC weather, I asked her why the policy change.

"This is a special case," she replied. "We have a terminal Vietnam veteran with only a few weeks to live who really wants to see the Wall."

"I'll do it."

"Okay, thanks. It's not a full-fledged Honor Flight, just you as an escort and the veteran and an RN in case there are any medical issues. I normally wouldn't do this but I doubt she will make it to our next scheduled flight."

Hmm, she. This would be the first female veteran I had escorted. I knew that women had served in all the wars that the United States had fought but they were still an under-recognized population. Most people assumed that the women were safe in noncombat roles since they weren't allowed to serve in that capacity until after the turn of the century. But not serving in a combat role really meant that they didn't receive training in what to do when a combat role was thrust upon them. I was looking forward to the things I could learn from this Veteran.

I arrived at the airport at the scheduled time and place to meet Meredith Fleming, the veteran and her nurse. As I approached the ticket counter I saw a woman in a wheelchair. She had an air of authority about her, that unmistakable sense of being someone who was used to giving orders and having them followed. I walked up to her and asked if she was Ms. Fleming.

"I am Colonel Fleming," she replied. "Or at least I was until I retired. I got my twenty years in and it was clear that I wasn't going any further so I retired and went to work for the VA. But I will answer faster to Colonel than Ms. so you should probably use that if you want to get my attention."

"It would be my honor to call you Colonel. I'm Devin and I have done a number of these honor flights, usually with a big crowd of people though."

"Well, if I am to call you Devin, then you must call me Meredith. I know there are usually lots of people on these things but this really came about at the last minute and is sort of outside of channels. I appreciate your willingness to make this happen on such short notice. I'm afraid that I haven't got long to live, advanced liver cancer, and I kept putting this trip off but I don't have much time left."

"It's my pleasure to escort you, and thank you for your service." I had thanked a lot of people for their service and it was never perfunctory. I was always cognizant of the fact that anyone who signed up for the military, or really anyone who served whether they volunteered or not, had been willing to give their life for the people of this country.

Just then a sleepy looking very young woman walked up to us, popping her gum and bopping her head, I presume in time to the music flooding the earbuds attached to her phone. She pulled a speaker out of one ear and asked if we were Devin and Meredith.

"I am Devin," I replied, pointing at myself. "And this is Colonel Fleming."

"Okay, cool. I'm Bethany. Let me know if you are feeling bad or need anything. You might have to tap me to get my attention as I will be listening to my music or actually sleeping once we get on the plane. Jeez, why did they have to schedule this flight so damn early?" With that she slipped the ear bud back in, sat down several feet away, and resumed her head bopping and gum popping.

Meredith and I just looked at each other, simultaneously shook our heads, and continued our conversation. We moved through security and boarded the plane. Normally the honor flights had crowds of people applauding when the veterans got off the plane in the DC airport. In fact, that was how I found out about Honor Flight. I was in the airport waiting for a flight when I heard cheers and applause coming from a few gates down. As the veterans deplaned, volunteers were there to cheer for them and thank them for their service. I found that this was particularly significant for the Vietnam veterans as they had not been cheered when they returned from war; in fact they had been vilified.

I asked Meredith what kind of reception she had when she returned from Vietnam.

"I didn't really pay attention to all that. There was certainly no one throwing us tickertape parades but I was so numb when I returned that I really didn't pay attention. I didn't know it then but it was probably some sort of PTSD."

"From what you had seen over there?"

"That was part of it. I was twenty-two years old. Except for attending nursing school, I had never been away from my home in Auburn, MI, a town of 2500 people. I joined the nursing corps and with only minimal training I was shipped over to Vietnam. Nothing could have prepared me for what I saw and felt and did, nothing at all, but the training and orientation I received was laughable. The weapons used by both sides were meant to cause the most possible damage and the helicopters got injured soldiers from the battlefield to us really fast. But because of that, we were dealing with damage and injuries of a scope never before seen."

She shifted in her airplane seat and grimaced.

"Are you in pain? Do you need the nurse or meds or anything?"

"No, the only pain is the memory of what those poor soldiers went through, the phosphorus, the Agent Orange, anti-personnel weapons. And me, at twenty-two, sticking my hand inside the body of an eighteen-year-old kid, trying to hold his organs in place so he could be sewn up. I swear, I grew up fast over there. After six months I was the old hand, the experienced one. That's when Ellen showed up. She looked as young and scared as I probably did just six months before. But, by then I was jaded and salty as hell, or so

I thought. But something about Ellen made me want to shelter her, to keep that look of wonder, or at least her sense of innocence, intact."

The flight attendant came by and asked if we wanted a drink or some peanuts. She virtually ignored Meredith as she leaned over to try and capture my attention. Don't get me wrong, I didn't mind a pretty woman flirting with me in an appropriate place and at the proper time (usually defined as when I could do something about it). I ignored her attempts at flirtation and focused my attention back on Meredith.

As the flight attendant moved on down the aisle, Meredith smacked me on the shoulder.

"Why didn't you at least ask for her number?"

I was pleasantly surprised that she was not upset about the obvious flirting between two women. Generally, on the honor flights my sexuality was not front and center. The generation of veterans I usually accompanied came from a time and place before gay pride, a time when people didn't share that kind of information, when gays were dishonorably discharged, at least when their specialty was not desperately needed by the powers that be. Those kinds of homosexuals were tolerated until their skills were no longer needed and then drummed out. Since I was there as a tour guide for the veterans I didn't share information about myself.

"Or do you have someone at home already and that's why you didn't make a move?"

"No, I'm single," I replied.

She smacked my shoulder again; it seemed that was her go to move. "Girl, when someone is sending out signals like that you have to strike while the iron is hot."

"No way. It's rude to the lady you are with if you flirt with someone else or as my father used to say, ya dance with who ya brung."

"Well, I appreciate the respect but seriously, you could have . . ."

"No need to finish that statement. What about you,? Anyone waiting at home?"

A flicker of something crossed her face. It passed so quickly I couldn't identify it, it was sadness and joy and anticipation all wound up into one.

"Remember I mentioned Ellen?" she asked.

"Oh oh. I knew there was something about the way you said her name."

"Slow down there. Yes, we were together back in 1966 when we were in-country. We were surrounded by so much violence and hatred that I think the love we shared was the only thing that kept me sane. I even questioned my belief in God over there. How could the God I believed in allow so much harm and damage and injury to happen to people?"

She must have seen something cross my face when she mentioned belief in God.

"Are you not a believer then?"

"There are times when I wished with all my heart that I could believe, when I think it would have been easier to believe there is a life after this one, times when I could have been comforted by the thought. I step right up to that edge, that wishing for the comfort of faith but I've never been able to cross the last barrier. I've never truly believed that we're more than what we have here and now."

"And what of the soul? Don't you think that's what makes us better than animals?"

I didn't sense any challenge in her voice, or worse yet, the tone of a person who had found an audience and was bound and determined to convert me to the one true faith, whatever religion she belonged to. "I think the soul is just a term for the best of our humanity, our aspirations and dreams of all that we could be if we lived to be our true loving and giving selves."

"Well, you're not here for me to convert so let me just say that the thing that has sustained me for the last forty-eight years is the thought of being reunited again with Ellen."

Just then the pilot's voice broke in over the intercom to tell us that we would be arriving soon and to prepare for arrival into Reagan National Airport. We landed and taxied to the terminal.

Generally the honor flights had huge tour buses to take our veterans to the memorial for the war they served in but this was a sort of cobbled together thing to accommodate Meredith so we just had a car service on call for the day. We exited the plane and headed for the baggage claim area to meet our driver. He stood holding a sign reading Colonel Fleming. We got our group loaded up and headed toward the National Mall.

December in DC could be tricky. Sometimes the weather was cold and snowy, or worse, everything could be covered in a thin sheen of ice which would make getting Meredith around in her wheelchair challenging. Fortunately today was a crisp fifty-five degrees with the sun shining and clear blue skies with a few puffy white clouds for contrast. As we approached the Wall, Meredith pointed to the memorial to the left and asked me what war that was. There were several statues of men in full combat gear spread out several feet apart from one another.

"That's the Korean War Memorial. It's probably my favorite one. It is especially poignant in the early morning when the fog clings to the ground. I think it looks like what it must have been like to be there."

I pushed her over closer and we sat in silence for a few minutes. I was lost in thought of war and the loss of life, both American and foreign and yet again wondered why, if there was a God, he allowed such human suffering.

"It's free will," Meredith said.

I started at the response to my inner monologue.

"Your face is an open book. I believe that God gave us free will and turned us loose, hoping that his creation would rise to the highest heights but also knowing that there was a possibility that lowest depths could be plumbed as well. If God were responsible for war, that would mean that we, you and I and everyone, had no real choices in our lives and no responsibility for our choices. C'mon, push me over to the Wall please."

We moved to the black wall with over 58,000 names inscribed on it. The names were in chronological order based on the day they died or went MIA. As we moved along the length of the wall it got taller until it met another wall at an angle and the size began decreasing. There was nothing on the wall but names and the sheer number was overwhelming. As we neared the end Meredith asked me to stop.

Close to the end of the wall, chronologically one of the last to die was the name Ellen Skyler. As Meredith lovingly stroked the name, I felt tears rolling down my cheeks. The Wall was built to reflect the image of whoever was in front of the memorial.

From my perspective it looked like Meredith was reaching out and touching another person. I started—for a moment it appeared that she was reaching out and touching a young woman in fatigues. The loving expression on the reflected face made me long for someone to look at me that way. I blinked and the reflection was Meredith but it easily could have been a reflection of her lost love, reaching across time and space to guide her home.

"She almost made it out. We had plans. We were going to move to New York where we could be together. She was going on a milk run, to get supplies to make sure the nurses coming after us had what they needed to carry on our work. She wasn't supposed to be on the chopper, it was supposed to be me. But I was packing my stuff to go home. We had a discharge date and flights scheduled."

As her thin hand, with prominent veins gently stroked the name on the wall and tears ran down her face, the full weight of her loss dropped on me. She had been without her love for forty-eight years. For longer than I had been alive, she had been waiting to be reunited with the one made for her.

She looked up at me, the lines of tears on her red cheeks and said to me, or maybe to Ellen, "It won't be long now."

As I got ready to push her back to the car I told her thank you. When she asked for what I replied, "I had no faith and I still don't have much but your deep and abiding belief that you would see Ellen again has given me a glimmer of it. It's not much but it's definitely there where it wasn't before."

"It doesn't have to be much, it can be as small as a mustard seed."

Karen Richard is a labor contract negotiator by day and author by night. She has held numerous jobs in her life from cook to mail carrier. She lives in the northeastern United States with her wife and their cats. She is a graduate of the University of Notre Dame Law School although she won't say what year. As a hint, it was the last year that the Fighting Irish won a national championship in football. She stands firm in the belief that, like the Phoenix, the Irish will rise from the ashes and reign as National Champions again! She has taken and passed the bar in Michigan, Maryland and Wisconsin, marking the only three times in her life she passed a bar without stopping in for a drink.